I0675723

DUMISAI

AND THE COVENANT OF THE ANCESTORS

Christopher R. Obie

Copyright © 2012 Christopher R. Obie

All rights reserved.

ISBN: 0-9718530-3-7
ISBN-13: 978-0-9718530-3-4

This book is a work of fiction. Any references to historical events, real people or real locales are used fictitiously. Other names, characters, places and incidents are the product of the author's imagination, and any resemblance to actual events or locales or persons, living or dead, is entirely coincidental.

DEDICATION

For Sondisa, Damani, Jasseim, and Chioneso...   thanks for the inspiration. Without your unrelenting urging for new and more imaginative adventures, this story would not have happened.

Carmen... thanks for your patience and support, and of course, for believing.

ACKNOWLEDGMENTS

Cover Art & Design by Derrick A. Richardson (Meki Ra Sa Men)

TABLE OF CONTENTS

Christopher R. Obie

PROLOGUE

Malaika winced in pain as the baby's head slowly emerged from her womb.

"Push!" Lueji instructed firmly. "It won't be long now."

Bento listened intently from around the corner of the hut, straining to check on the progress of his wife while the old man briefly paused between drumming. As the beating of the drum resumed, firmly establishing the rhythm, the other drummers joined in with Baba Kenje in a ritual song to help the birthing process along.

"Oohhh…!!" Malaika groaned. This time loud enough for Bento to hear over the drum beat and chorus of men singing.

"It's a boy!" Lueji exclaimed excitedly.

Bento raced over to his wife as quickly as he could.

"Look, Poppa," Lueji instructed, "you have a fine baby boy."

Bento carefully took the newborn from the woman, cuddling him in his arms. He whispered some tender words in his son's ear.

"Let me see my son," Malaika demanded softly.

"Here, honey, here he is. You did good," Bento comforted as he handed the baby to his wife.

"He is so beautiful. Such big, bright eyes," she cooed, "Bento, what shall we call him?"

"We will choose a name that fits," Bento reminded, "after observing him for a few days as is our custom."

"Look how tightly he grips my finger," Jabulani remarked after placing his drum aside and extending his hands in a request to hold the child. "He is going to be a strong little fellow." Jabulani lifted his godson away from its mother, carefully cradling the infant close to his chest. As the gathering looked on, absorbed in the celebratory mood, only Bento noticed the shocked look that suddenly crossed Jabulani's face. Jabulani stood motionless, his facial expression frozen with a look of disbelief.

"Jabulani... Jabulani!" Bento called worriedly, immediately focusing everyone's attention directly onto his best friend. "What's wrong, man? You look like you've seen a ghost!"

"No," Jabulani replied as if slowly emerging from some hypnotic spell. "No, that's not it at all. Didn't you hear? Didn't you hear the child speak?"

Bento rushed to his friend to retrieve his newborn son, "Naw, man... what's wrong with you? This is a brand new baby. He just got here. He can't speak!"

"No, he did speak," Jabulani insisted. "He told me that my livestock was sick. He said it needs my attention."

Everyone looked at Jabulani, their concern for his sanity clearly evident on their faces.

"Don't look at me like that. I'm just telling you what I heard."

"Aay!" interjected Baba Kenje attempting to rescue the celebration from what was quickly becoming a somber occasion. "Time for some music, ehh!" He quickly beat out a rhythm associated with celebrations and was joined by all the drummers except Jabulani. Bento's friend was not only visibly disturbed by what he had experienced with the infant, he was embarrassed by the people's reaction to him. As the music played on into the evening, he left the gathering inconspicuously, attempting to avoid drawing any additional attention to himself.

Jabulani's knock on the door of Bento's hut sounded full of exasperation. It had been nearly a week since the birth of his best friend's infant son, but it was obvious that he was anxious about something as he pounded the door, refusing to be ignored.

"Hey, take it easy. I'm coming... I'm coming already," Bento answered.

As Bento opened the door, he could see that Jabulani was obviously flustered and upset.

"Jabulani, what's wrong, man? We haven't seen you since the baby arrived."

"I know Bento, I didn't want to upset you and Malaika again, but I have to show you something. Can you come with me?"

"Okay," Bento agreed, after seeing his friend's level of anxiety. "Malaika, honey, I'll be back shortly."

After walking for several minutes, the men eventually approached Jabulani's hut.

"Why can't you just tell me what it is we're going to see?" Bento queried.

"No, you have to see this for yourself," Jabulani insisted.

As they made their way to the back of the hut, Bento stopped dead in his tracks.

"What happened, man?!! Your goats... they're dead! That's nearly half of your herd!"

"Yes, thirteen to be exact. Thirteen of my finest goats—dead," Jabulani pointed out.

"Well, what happened? Did someone poison them?"

"The baby, Bento, this is what he was talking about."

"No, that's crazy talk, man. My baby didn't do this."

"Bento, listen to me—I'm not saying he did it. He just warned me about it. You've got to believe me. The very next day after I heard him speak, they just started dying. Nothing I did seemed to help. I'm telling you, Bento, your son has the *gift of sight.*"

"No, I don't believe it."

"You think I would make this up, Bento? You think I would kill my own livestock?"

"No, I'm not saying that. I don't know what to think."

"Listen, Bento, you are like my brother. I wouldn't lie to you, especially about something like this. All I'm saying is that your son is special. That's nothing to be afraid of. Look, among my people, the *Ndebele,* we have a name for a child such as yours: *Dumisai.* It means one who is a *Herald of the Future.*

"Okay, Jabulani, I just need some time to think about this, that's all," Bento concluded, his attention still focused on the dead goats. "And Jabulani...," Bento added, turning to face his friend with his hand extended, "thanks, brother. I'm glad that you're my friend."

1: Beginnings

Dumisai sat on the ground with his legs crossed, his eyes scanning the treetops in search of the animal whose fidgeting had caused a soft stirring among the leaves.

"Probably just another squirrel," he thought to himself. Still, the uncertainty of not knowing only fueled his curiosity. Upon hearing the rustling among the leaves again, Dumisai stretched forward his neck in an effort to locate the source of the soft, fluttering noise.

"There!" he whispered excitedly, pointing to a cluster of tree branches after noticing a slight movement among the leaves. After maneuvering to get a clearer view, Dumisai saw two squirrels frolicking near the top of a large oak tree. His curiosity satisfied, he smiled as he repositioned himself in the spot that he had made comfortable for sitting, allowing the squirrels' playfulness to briefly entertain him. He watched as the little creatures scrambled about the tree playing with each other, jumbling an acorn which had become the object of their game. Their playful banter continued unabated until they managed to dislodge a small sum of nuts that they had previously collected and stored in the tree. Dumisai watched with interest as the squirrels temporarily stopped their playful activity and quickly made their way down to the ground in an effort to retrieve the spilt goodies. Meticulously, they grabbed up each of the scattered acorns, returning them one by one to their storage nest near the top of the tree. The determination of the squirrels working toward their objective held Dumisai's attention. He noticed that a few of the nuts had rolled by a large opening at the base of the tree trunk. Realizing that a portion of their bounty had found its way into the tree opening, the squirrels cautiously approached the base of the tree, stopping just short of the cavity containing the remaining acorns. Dumisai laughed under his breath as he silently watched the squirrels contemplating their next move. After staring into the darkness of the tree hollow for several seconds, the bushy-tailed rodents abandoned the idea of retrieving the additional acorns and instead scampered back to their nest to inspect what they had already collected.

Dumisai thought it was strange how the squirrels had abandoned the nuts left by tree and before long, decided to investigate the hollowed out tree cavity for himself. Peering into the opening, he couldn't see anything except for a black fog which completely engulfed the inside of the tree trunk. As he continued to gaze into the impenetrable darkness, Dumisai was struck by an eerie feeling that came over him. The darkness of the tree cavity seemed to have an unnatural quality to it. The more he stared into it, the stranger it appeared. It was as if the darkness itself was moving, swirling continuously in a circular motion. Fascinated, Dumisai succumbed to his curiosity. He was drawn to the swirling movement of the dark matter within the tree as if it had him hypnotized. Fearlessly, he poked his head into the tree cavity while secretly hoping to discover some well protected secret contained within it. His head was barely past the edge of the opening, however, when he heard a voice calling him from a distance. It was ever so faint, but still clear enough to shock Dumisai back to his senses.

"Grandmother…?" he muttered to himself while quickly retrieving his head out of the tree trunk. Dumisai stepped back bewildered as the realization that his Grandmother Lueji was already deceased reentered his awareness. He looked around briefly for something to either confirm or disprove his suspicions even though he knew that she couldn't possibly be there. Still, her voice had been so unmistakable that he was sure it must have been her unless he was either hearing things or his mind was playing tricks on him. If it truly had been her, then she could have only been there as spirit. The idea of his grandmother present in a ghostly form was a little unsettling. Dumisai quickly gathered his personal items and hurried away from the area. Once he was far enough away and able to settle his nerves, he walked to the river where he found a nice spot to sit and collect his thoughts.

The incident at the tree had triggered a flood of thoughts and memories about his Grandmother Lueji. The two of them had been very close before her death and his memories of her always initially left him feeling sad. Usually though, with a little effort, Dumisai was able to block out the accompanying feelings of sadness and concentrate instead on the memories that he was fond of. He still missed the times that he and his grandmother used to spend talking, her sharing old *home stories*, and him asking a thousand questions in an attempt to gain a clear understanding of the *old ways*—the African traditions that had been passed down over several generations. Her stories had always stirred a longing in him for Africa, and he often wondered why the family had left the place that was so endeared to them. Lueji had tried to explain the circumstances that led to the family's flight out of Angola. She told him how the country had quickly descended into chaos once the civil war began. *UNITA* rebels had marched into their village, forcing the people to flee their homes and leave their belongings behind in order to avoid certain capture and possibly even death. Since most of the villagers had been staunch supporters of the revolutionary government installed by the *MPLA*, they were very fortunate to make it to safety across the border into neighboring Zambia. From there the group of refugees eventually decided to make the perilous trip across the Atlantic Ocean to the United States. They had heard stories about America and how it represented a land full of opportunity. It was a place where they could put away something for the future while waiting out the war, but since there was no visible end to the fighting in sight, Lueji and the other elders decided to pool their monies and purchase a small tract of land in the American southwest. They chose a small farm in southeast Oklahoma which was far removed from most modern conveniences and modeled it after their village in Angola.

As the war continued to claim its victims, more expatriates would cross the Atlantic and find their way to the little settlement in Oklahoma. Eventually, a small village emerged and emigrants from other parts of Africa also joined the newly formed community of Africans in America. Even though the other villagers were small in number and had come from different ethnic groups on the continent, they found that they shared many similarities in their spiritual beliefs and cultural traditions, and therefore could easily come together to form a community. Among these new world villagers were Dumisai's mother, Malaika, who was visibly pregnant at the time, and his father, Bento, who was eager to provide a safe and nurturing home for his soon to be firstborn son. In the twelve years since that fateful journey Dumisai had managed to maintain his African identity intact, taking advantage of the sacrifices made by his grandmother and the other elders. Their persistent efforts had succeeded in instilling a worldview that would serve him well throughout the rest of his life.

At twelve, Dumisai was the oldest child in the Oklahoma settlement which his elders affectionately called *'Little Angola'*. Being at least five years older than every other child in the settlement, he had learned to be content by keeping to himself and often deliberately avoided certain village functions. Dumisai liked to wander off by himself to observe nature and the surrounding environment. He was fascinated by the natural world and found that he could approach certain animals, including many that other people purposely avoided. He usually left the village around mid-morning and would stay gone for most of the day, sometimes becoming so engrossed in observing the interactions of the different animals that he would completely lose track of the time. Eventually, he was able to cultivate a special rapport with the animals that he enjoyed watching so much, sharing his snacks when he had it to offer with the animals that allowed him to get close enough to do so. Dumisai thrived in the woods surrounded by nature and all the creatures of the wild. It was there that he felt the most comfortable and free of the problems associated with the world.

Dumisai inhaled the warm mid-morning air charged by the invisible rays of the sun. As he ventured to one of his favorite spots in the woods, a soft breeze gently caressed his skin causing the nearly undetectable growth of hair on his arms to stand on end and reveal tiny goose bumps prickling across his forearm. He stopped in a clearing just beyond the wooded area which separated his village from the river and looked into the clear sky, taking a moment to absorb the warmth of the sun's rays beating down on his brown skin. Everything was peaceful all around him, yet something in the air felt different. Dumisai could not quite place the feeling that he was experiencing but paused to check his surroundings. Immediately, he heard a series of high-pitched shrieks overhead which caused his attention to shift upward. There were three hawks circling above like vultures eyeing some doomed prey. They circled at different altitudes but appeared to be flying in a formation, each almost equally spaced in distance from the others. The sight of the hawks circling above captivated his attention, leaving him standing fixed in place unable to take his eyes away from the spectacle. Finally, the hawks flew away together, but they had flown only about fifty yards when they stopped and began circling again. Compelled by curiosity, Dumisai followed the birds. As he approached the perimeter of their circle they flew away again and then stopped after several more yards only to resume their circling activity with a series of shrill shrieks. The actions of the hawks seemed purposefully designed to provoke Dumisai into following them. He soon found himself running just trying to keep pace with the birds, allowing himself to be led further and further away from the village. Just as he realized that he was completely lost, he saw each of the hawks perch in a nearby tree. Dumisai slowly walked toward the birds, being careful not to scare them away. As he approached the closest of the three, a loud thunderclap suddenly boomed overhead, shattering the quiet peace of the outdoor landscape and spooking each of the birds. Dumisai looked up toward the heavens but found it to be completely clear of any clouds. The strange chain of events caused him to wonder if he had imagined the whole episode. Frustrated, he decided to begin looking for a route back to the village. He knew that he had to find his way back before the setting sun abandoned him to the darkness of night. As he searched for a possible trail back home, the wind picked up in intensity, resulting in a breeze which was becoming increasingly more difficult to ignore. The wind swirled about his head, whistling softly past his ears until he stopped momentarily and trained his concentration on the soft windsong that was serenading him. Perhaps he was daydreaming, experiencing some mild state of trance, but he was sure that he could hear his name being spoken from a distance. The experience was exhilarating, further mesmerizing the child. He listened closer, now convinced that he could hear his name being spoken. It was faint, almost indistinguishable from the wind itself, but Dumisai carefully trained his ears on the soft, lilting melody until it began to come through clearly, sounding more and more like someone calling out to him. The gentle call of the voice continued, annunciating each syllable of his name slowly and softly.

"Yes," Dumisai answered, his response barely audible. "I am Dumisai." The words floated effortlessly from his lips, almost as if they were being pulled out of him without his conscious awareness.

"DOO – MEE – SAI – EE," whispered the gentle voice, *"YOUR AN-CES-TORS HAVE RE-TURNED ON THE LIPS OF THE WIND TO SUM-MON YOU."*

The soft whispers serenading his ears gently carried away his thoughts, leaving in its wake the mesmerizing effect of a spellbinding charm. Dumisai could only listen in his present state of mental suspension. His attempt to respond was muted as he fixed his mouth to formulate words that would not verbalize.

"YOUR HEART IS PURE LIT-TLE DU-MI-SAI, FOL-LOW IT FOR IT WILL NOT LEAD YOU A-STRAY. IF YOU DO THIS, GREAT WILL BE YOUR FOR-TUNE. YOU ARE THE ONE WHOM THE AN-CES-TORS HAVE EN-TRUST-ED WITH A SPE-CIAL GIFT... THE 'GIFT OF GREAT CON-SE-QUENCE'."

"Gift of Consequence...?" Dumisai mumbled, finally managing to regain control of his ability to speak. "What's a *'Gift of Consequence'*?"

"ALL THAT YOU NEED TO KNOW NOW IS THAT THIS IS A 'GIFT' THAT COMES FROM THE CRE-A-TOR OF ALL THINGS, AND ITS POW-ER MUST ON-LY BE USED FOR GOOD. IF YOU A-BUSE THE POW-ER THAT HAS BEEN PLACED IN YOUR CARE, IT WILL BE TA-KEN AWAY AND GONE FOR-EV-ER."

"Why me...?" Dumisai asked half-dazed, yet a little less anxious now that he had found his voice. "What if I don't want this *Gift*?"

This time there was no answer. The silence shocked Dumisai back to his senses. The air was still now, as if it had been that way all day long. The boy looked around at his surroundings, attempting to locate anything that seemed out of the ordinary. There was no trace of the hawks which had been flying overhead, nor was anything else out of place. Dumisai let out a big sigh and then turned to begin the long trek back to the village. The sun was starting to set and he didn't want to get caught out in the dark, especially since he did not know exactly where he was at. As he began to walk, he realized that even though he had been lost, the way home suddenly seemed obvious as if he had walked the area many times before.

Dumisai's mind stayed fixed on the strange experience all the way home. What did it really mean? Was it even real, or had he just imagined the whole episode? He tried to shake off the strange feeling which had accompanied the experience of being spoken to by the wind but his head was still in a whirlwind. The flux of mental energies swirling in his head would not allow his mind to become settled. Every thought that came harkened back to the *'Gift of Great Consequence'*, leading him to wonder about what *powers* it potentially represented. It was impossible to focus on anything. He finally abandoned any hope of making sense of the situation. Instead, he reasoned that once he got back home, he could get some sleep and maybe be able to sort through his thoughts the next day.

Dumisai's mother and father were worried sick about him. He had never stayed gone away for so long and a small crowd gathered in front of the village to offer comfort to his parents while discussing the formation of a search party. When Dumisai finally arrived, it was dark but his mother immediately recognized his approaching form silhouetted against the backdrop of the waxing moon. The boy immediately apologized to everyone for causing such concern among the people of the village. His parents were thrilled by his safe return but his father shot him a stern look of reproach before offering a hug. Without another word being spoken it was clear that everyone was waiting for an explanation. Dumisai mentioned only that he was not hungry and asked for permission to return to his hut. Taking their cue from the boy's parents, the crowd agreed reluctantly, after seeing that the boy was exhausted and probably had not eaten much that day. Dumisai quickly took advantage of everyone's concurrence before they had a chance to reconsider, and then retired to his parent's hut for the evening.

2: Discovery

Dumisai sat up quickly, awakened suddenly by the events in his dream. He looked around anxiously, attempting to verify his whereabouts as he waited for his eyes to adjust to the darkness of the room. His sheets were damp, drawing his attention to the bed. Slowly, he recognized the structure that he was sitting on and the surrounding space that was his room. The familiarity put his mind at ease while simultaneously confirming that he was simply recovering from a bad dream. The sweat-drenched bed sheets were an indication of just how intense the dream had been. Dumisai could remember being chased through the forest but could not recall any additional details of the dream. As he strained to remember more, he was sure that it was the same nightmare that had been haunting him for the past several weeks. He lay in bed staring at the ceiling as he contemplated the different possible meanings. The fact that the nightmare seemed to be occurring more regularly concerned him. He lay back down in an attempt to relax but the jumble of thoughts combined with adrenaline made it impossible to fall back asleep. Frustrated, Dumisai resigned himself to getting an early start on the day and simply exited the bed.

After washing up, Dumisai got dressed and grabbed something to eat prior to completing his chores. Once his work was done, he began his walk through the woods. By the time he was half-way to his destination, all thoughts of the dream had faded into oblivion. He ventured down to the edge of the river where he could count on the soothing calm of the water to help him sort through all the events that he had recently experienced. There were so many ideas racing through his head that it was no wonder he was lost in his thoughts well before he even reached the river. He replayed the events of the previous day in an attempt to come to grips with the experience. "What if it had all been real?" he mumbled under his breath. "It *would* be neat to have some special power that no one else has." Convinced that the entire episode must have been some wild daydream, Dumisai laughed out loud, amused at himself for actually entertaining such a foolish fantasy. Enjoying the moment while it lasted, he thought it would be fun to play the game out to completion. Eyeing a rock about the size of a grapefruit, Dumisai stopped and pointed to the stone making it the focus of his concentration and then slowly lifted his hand as if commanding the stone to rise. Nothing happened. He doubled his efforts, secretly hoping that his previous day's experience had indeed been real. The rock still would not move. Dumisai became frustrated by the stone's lack of cooperation before finally giving up. His frustration caused him realize that he was taking the entire episode more seriously than he had been willing to admit to himself. Embarrassed by the prospect that someone could have actually seen him acting as though he really believed in something so silly, he cautiously looked around to make sure that no one had been watching. Satisfied that he was alone, Dumisai breathed a sigh of relief before proceeding on his way to the river.

Upon reaching the riverbank, Dumisai spotted some flat stones that had accumulated over time on the shore. He liked to skip rocks to see how far he could make them skid on top of the water. Picking up a perfectly smooth, flat stone, he slung it spinning toward the river. The rock skidded cleanly across the water's surface before finally sinking to the watery depths below. As Dumisai watched, he couldn't help but be reminded of the obvious power that he exercised over the stones. Sure it wasn't extraordinary, yet a certain amount of power was required to be able to physically lift and propel the stones. Besides, he reasoned, life made more sense following this arrangement. At least he was able to understand what was happening as he hurled the stones across the river.

After exhausting all of the flat stones in his immediate vicinity, Dumisai continued walking along the riverbank when he noticed a small animal in the brush. His curiosity was piqued as he attempted to get close enough to determine exactly what kind of animal it was. He could hear it scurrying around, apparently trying to hide among the shrubs. Dumisai stepped cautiously, trying hard to avoid frightening the creature away. As he got closer he could see that it was a very small rabbit cowering behind a thicket of bushes. The boy gently pushed aside the twigs to see the frightened rabbit close-up. Maybe it would realize that he intended no harm towards it if he offered the animal some food, he reasoned. As he reached into his bag to get some fruit, the rabbit tried scampering from the cover of the bushes in a desperate attempt to escape. It only managed to get a couple feet beyond the bush cover in its panic to get away due to an obvious injury inhibiting its ability to hop freely. Dumisai could see that one of its feet was badly injured. Trying his best not to further frighten the little critter, he watched it at first, concluding that the rabbit could not have been much more than a few months old. Slowly, he walked around to the front of the kitten to offer it some fruit. Somewhat skeptical and still afraid, the rabbit stretched forward to cautiously nibble at the fruit in the boy's outstretched hand before finally grabbing it with its teeth. Dumisai kept offering small portions, each a little closer to himself than the last and all the while gently coaxing the injured animal in a re-assuring tone until he was finally able to touch the rabbit with one hand while feeding it a small piece of fruit with the other. As he stroked the back of the animal's ear, the rabbit seemed less inhibited and nudged closer to the young boy. Dumisai seized the opportunity to pick up the bunny and tenderly caress it, but as soon as he held the small animal in his hands he noticed a faint glow beginning to radiate outwards, completely encircling the creature. At first the light emanating from within his cupped hands startled the boy, causing him to nearly drop the injured bunny, but he quickly gathered his wits and gently sat the rabbit back on the ground and then watched as it hopped around freely. It was amazing. Dumisai's mind was racing trying to make sense of what had just happened when he looked up and saw several more animals walking towards him.

The sight of all the animals approaching caught Dumisai off guard. He instinctively took a couple steps backward in order to put some more distance between himself and the approaching animals. He quickly surveyed the area on all sides. There were many animals of different species approaching yet none appeared threatening. Dumisai silently breathed a sigh of relief. As he waited to see what would happen, he managed to quickly count about twenty, but that was less than half of all the animals approaching from his side of the river. Some of the animals amongst the group were buffalo as well as several deer. Dumisai also noticed a few rabbits, including the one he had just helped, plus a black bear, some coyote, and a mountain lion among the grouping. Several different species of birds had perched in a tree nearby to where the animals had almost encircled the boy. Dumisai was not afraid—he had always enjoyed a special relationship with animals—but he could not help but feel uneasy. They came within a couple yards of him before each animal slowly kneeled down onto the knees of its front legs. Dumisai stood frozen in his stance while attempting to keep an eye on all the animals in the semi-circle which had formed around him. As he looked around, he established eye contact with several of the animals in the front of the group. A realization came to him suddenly. Without understanding how he knew, he was sure that they wanted to tell him something. Something important. It was as though he could suddenly sense the urgency of their thoughts and knew that they had come to convey a message to him. A sense of excitement began to build as he slowly looked around, taking time to look at each of the animals. They appeared to be completely silent, yet Dumisai was sure that he was hearing their thoughts. He listened closely to the animals excitedly chattering as if they were talking amongst each other, communicating by mental means. Dumisai continued to stare, fascinated by the gathering while attempting to make sense of the mental chatter he was hearing in his head. Looking up, he noticed a large black raven which appeared to be exerting its leadership over the other birds in a nearby tree.

"Be still," the raven asserted to the other birds perched in the tree, *"and show some respect."*

"Hey you…?" Dumisai called, surprised at himself for actually attempting to talk to an animal. "You birds up in the tree, are you able to understand my words as I understand yours?"

"Yes, Dumisai," replied the large black raven, *"we are able to understand you and we can project our thoughts into your mind as well."*

"How is that possible?" Dumisai questioned again, attempting to assure himself that he was actually dialoging with an animal.

"You have the Gift, my friend. Do not be afraid—it seems that you have been chosen to do a great work while on the earth," the raven replied.

"The *Gift*…? What is this *Gift* that I keep hearing about?" Dumisai questioned, recalling the term from the events of the previous day.

"You were chosen to receive the 'Gift of Great Consequence' which has now been passed on to you by your ancestors. You were chosen because your heart is pure and good, and because your ancestors know of your desire for balance in the universe," the raven replied. *"The Gift is only given to one who is worthy and you are the first to wield its power in many generations."*

"How do *you* know this…? How do you know me?" Dumisai interrogated further, the implication of what he was hearing finally settling in on him.

"We animals are in harmony with Creation and therefore are privileged to know these things, for the Creator who is all-knowing dwells in each of us."

"Does not the Creator also dwell in me and all humans as well?" inquired Dumisai.

"You are correct Dumisai," interjected a mountain lion rising from his kneeled position to join in the dialogue, *"the Creator does dwell in all living things, but most humans are ignorant of their Divinity and misuse the talents that God has given them to arrogantly mistreat the rest of Creation, causing the universe to be thrown out of balance."*

"I don't understand what all this means. Why did you come?" Dumisai inquired, now shifting his attention to the mountain lion. "Is there something that you need from me?"

"Yes, Dumisai," the mountain lion replied, *"the world is a very troubled place right now because of Man's arrogance and insensitivity. You were entrusted with the Gift to help bring the universe back into balance and to help the human family correct its destructive ways. With this power which has been entrusted to you, you will be able to accomplish things beyond the means of ordinary humans. Use it wisely and only for just cause. You were chosen because within you is a great respect for the earth and all of her creatures. Remain true to yourself and the teachings of your ancestors that have been passed down to you by your parents and the people of the village, and you will not fail."*

"What if I don't want that responsibility," Dumisai asked, hesitant to accept the burden implied by the words being communicated to him.

"Dumisai," the mountain lion insisted, *"it is your destiny."*

The animals all quickly rose to their feet. The raven spoke again: *"We came to you, Dumisai, in humble submission, for you are the one whom it has been prophesized will come and help lead the wayward human family back to its Divinity. As you go about your work, know that we will always be close by and will answer your call when you need us."*

The animals then turned and walked away, each going its own separate way as if nothing out of the ordinary had occurred. Dumisai watched as they dispersed before also turning to leave. As he looked over his shoulder one final time to watch the animals disappear into the landscape, he knew that the life he had come to know would never be the same. The thought stirred a nervous excitement inside him which caused his heartbeat to slightly quicken. He offered a guarded smile without allowing himself to get too excited. There was still a lot of uncertainty about his future, yet somehow, he knew that everything was going to be okay.

3: Confirmation

The midday sun shined mercilessly down on the village, forcing Dumisai to seek out a spot of shade near his parent's hut before taking time to order his thoughts. After locating a place of refuge from the scorching sun, he paced back and forth while constantly replaying the day's events in his mind. He recognized the seriousness of the responsibility that had been placed upon him but still struggled to keep his excitement in check. With everything that had happened, he knew that he was being called upon to do something special in the world and did not want to let anyone down. After managing to finally settle his thoughts, Dumisai concluded that he needed to get the advice of someone who would be able to counsel him on the best course of action going forward. He knew that his father was away at work in a nearby town and that his mother had ventured into the town to do some shopping, but his impatience would not allow him to sit and wait for their return. He decided to seek out one of the village elders instead and went looking for an old man named Kenje Kaleji.

Baba Kenje, as he was affectionately known, was a thin, wiry man with closely cropped white hair and a medium length, white beard. Despite his age, Baba Kenje was quick-witted and could be long-winded at times, but he commanded a great deal of respect from his peers who sat on the *Council of Elders*. His wisdom was legendary among the villagers, mainly due to his ability to win arguments by using one's own words against them while proving his point. He often used his position among the other elders to influence the outcome of council meetings and frequently led the discussions. Dumisai was comfortable around Baba Kenje because the elder always made an effort to maintain a friendly disposition and often took on the responsibility of keeping the mood light by making everyone laugh, especially during times when matters were very serious. Even though he had a knack for interjecting a good laugh at the appropriate time, he was still able to command the respect of the other council members for they knew that he was not one to neglect tradition. Dumisai wisely calculated that Baba Kenje would be the best person to talk to, but he also realized that the task of convincing the elder could prove to be difficult if the old man found his story to be too far-fetched. Unsure how Baba Kenje would respond to his tale, he knew that he at least had to try. Dumisai looked all over the settlement for the elder before finally finding him at the edge of the village collecting some medicinal herbs. Baba Kenje liked to chew on a stalk of sugar cane and caught a glimpse of Dumisai approaching as he spit out a portion of the cane juice.

"Hey, Dumisai!" he called, noticing a look of uncertainty on the boy's face as he arrived. "What brings you here, my boy?"

Dumisai approached slowly, attempting to be respectful as he had been taught.

"Baba Kenje, excuse me for interrupting," he stated as he kneeled in a gesture signifying that he was requesting permission to speak.

"Go ahead, son," the old man asserted as he nodded approvingly, signaling for Dumisai to rise. "Don't make me wait for my next lifetime. Spit it out, boy... what's troubling you?"

Upon standing, Dumisai began explaining the events of the past couple days in detail. As he talked, Kenje listened intently without interrupting, his right eyebrow raised slightly higher than normal to indicate his keen interest in the topic. Once Dumisai had finished speaking, Baba Kenje stared at him in silence for a few seconds longer, his eyes squinting now as if he was mulling over his thoughts. After a few moments more of the unusual silence which indicated that he was still contemplating what he had heard, the old man spit out a large amount of cane juice.

"Stay here!" he stated, the typical happy-go-lucky attitude now missing from his voice. "I will return shortly."

Without hesitation, Baba Kenje began walking back toward the village. He moved slowly at first, using the staff which he carried with him for leverage due to some stiffness in his joints. Once the old man got going, however, his stride picked up noticeably and he wasn't forced to rely on the stick as much. Dumisai had gotten a good look at it over the years, often focusing on its elaborate carvings. Its intricate designs were an indication that it belonged to someone of importance. He remembered his parents mentioning it in their conversations at times, remarking how the old stick had been passed down for many generations before finally being received by Baba Kenje. Watching the elder as he slowly disappeared into the woods, Dumisai was convinced that he had sought out the right person. He was also feeling pretty confident that he had made a good case to the elder because Baba Kenje had appeared to be very receptive to his story.

As his wait dragged on, Dumisai's optimistic thoughts slowly began to turn into questions. He had been sitting patiently now for nearly an hour and wondered why he hadn't been allowed to simply accompany Baba Kenje instead of waiting out at the edge of the woods for him to return. Then, after a few minutes more, Dumisai finally caught a glimpse of the old man returning through the woods. Looking closer, he could also see that someone else had joined Baba Kenje on his return journey. The person accompanying the elder looked to be small by comparison while walking beside the tall, gangly old man. As the two got closer, Dumisai could see that it was a woman. She was also an elder, yet Dumisai had only seen her close-up on very few occasions. He did not know very much about her, but he knew enough to realize that her presence made him very uncomfortable. She was old and her body was somewhat twisted and bent, apparently from some childhood disease or birth defect. She also had a stick which she carried with her like Baba Kenje, but unlike the old man, she was forced to rely on her crooked, yet sturdy staff to support her weight as she rambled forward.

Baba Kenje walked slowly, apparently allowing the bent-over body of the old woman an opportunity to keep pace with his long strides. Dumisai could clearly see now why the old man's return had taken so long. The woman moved slowly, laboriously shifting her weight from her one strong leg over to the walking stick, and then back to her strong leg again. Her skin was a pale, milky white complexion, owing to a rare occurrence in nature called albinism. Her white hair was dreadlocked and hung freely, almost reaching down to her shoulders in length. Draped over her upper body was a mostly-blue wrap-around fabric styled in traditional African print which contrasted sharply against her skin and accentuated her lack of pigmentation. Despite his best efforts to remain non-judgmental, the woman's appearance frightened the boy. He had heard that albinos were spiritual mediums and possessed powers beyond those of *ordinary* people. Because of her reputation as someone who worked with occult forces, Dumisai had always made an effort to avoid venturing too close to her hut whenever he went on his walks in the woods. Sometimes his curiosity would cause him to watch her from a distance as she participated in council meetings, but he was always careful to avoid being detected, afraid that her eyes, which were pink and distant, would freeze his body stiff if he was ever caught staring. Another thing that he thought to be odd was the fact that he had rarely ever heard the woman speak. In fact, he could not remember her uttering a single word unless some question had been put directly to her, and then her answers were always short, typically "yes" or "no" and accompanied by a head nod for emphasis. The people of the village knew her as *Ol' Manzalele*. She was a diviner and knew how to talk to the spirits of the dead. The stories that Dumisai had heard about her seemed strange and only added to his intimidation. As she approached with Baba Kenje, his heart began to beat a little faster for he knew that she was only consulted outside of the council under very serious circumstances.

As the two elders arrived to the spot where Dumisai was waiting, the old woman began to circle the boy slowly without uttering a word, as if looking for some detail that was out of place. Her actions made Dumisai even more uncomfortable than he already was but he dared not move an inch. Finally after several minutes, Manzalele completed her inspection and then looked toward the old man and nodded as if confirming something between the two of them. Dumisai did not know what was happening, but he was too terrified to interrupt and try to find out. The old woman, now finished with what she had come for, stepped to the side as a signal to Baba Kenje to begin explaining to the boy exactly what was occurring. The male elder stepped forward, quietly clearing his throat before beginning to speak.

"Long ago," he began cautiously, "back in our homeland before the White man came, a spiritual *Diviner* known as Niangi received a vision foretelling the coming of someone who would be great in the history of our people."

Baba Kenje's voice was naturally higher than most of the other men in the village, yet his tone would occasionally rise even higher when he got excited, especially when he wanted to emphasize a particular point. He also tended to get animated when speaking, often utilizing his hands to help get his point across. Still, his engaging personality allowed the younger people in the village see him as someone who was more approachable than the other elders. Now, however, the old man's usual display of levity was nowhere to be found as Dumisai noticed the seriousness of Baba Kenje's tone while he was being addressed by the elder.

"The story of that vision has been passed down for generations now," the old man continued. "It speaks of one who would come from among us and possess an extraordinary power." Baba Kenje paused briefly as though he was attempting to carefully choose the next words to come out of his mouth. "The story also states that this one will have to leave us in order to fulfill his destiny. Of course, there are those among us who have always maintained that the story was only a myth, but some of us, like Ol' Manzalele here, knew better. She has seen that the time was drawing near for the fulfillment of this prophecy and she has been trying to prepare us for its coming. Because of her insistence, we already have the subject under discussion in our council meetings. And now she has confirmed that it is you, Dumisai. You are the one that the prophecy speaks of. You are the one that the ancestors have entrusted with the '*Gift*.'"

Not wanting to overwhelm the boy with too much information, the elder paused to provide Dumisai with an opportunity to respond. The boy quickly interjected, seizing on the moment to speak.

"So you already knew?"

"Yes, Dumisai, we have been expecting this for a while now. We only needed confirmation and you have given us that," Baba Kenje admitted.

"Baba, why me? Why was I chosen?"

"We all are called by God to do his Will, son, but along the way there are choices that we must make. Because you have chosen to live truth, you yourself have done the choosing."

"How can I know what is required of me?"

"You have to trust what you have been taught, son. Everything that you have learned has been to prepare you for what is to come."

"You said that the prophecy states that I must leave?" Dumisai queried apprehensively.

"Yes, son, that is true. The fact that you have been made aware of your *Gift* means that the time has come for it to be put to its intended use."

"What about my mother... what about my family?"

"You need not worry about that, Dumisai. The village will take care of your family."

Dumisai was comforted by the elder's reassurance of his family's well-being, but was still unsure of his own future.

"How long then, before I have to leave?"

"I believe it will have to be sometime soon, son, for time is of the essence. Now that you know that you have a job to do, the sooner you get started, the better."

Dumisai was expressionless as he attempted to absorb the full meaning of Baba Kenje's words. It had become obvious that the *Gift* would have a profound effect on his future and would not simply be something to set him apart from other people.

"I'm sorry Dumisai, I know this is a lot to ask of you, but the ancestors have spoken and they know better than us when it comes to these things," the old man insisted, his voice now firmly established in his conviction. "You will soon be a man and as such, your responsibility must first be to the village as a whole, and in your case, your responsibilities will be even greater than that of the average person."

Baba Kenje paused momentarily as if his train of thought had been rudely interrupted by a sudden revelation.

"I do have a concern though," the old man resumed. "You have not yet gone through initiation. We would be remiss in our duty to send a boy out to do a job that's required of a man. Isn't that right, Manzalele?"

The old woman slowly nodded her agreement.

"Dumisai," Baba Kenje continued, "we must make the necessary arrangements for you to undergo your manhood rites. You are the first in this village that needs to go through such a program, and now that we have been caught laying down on the job, perhaps the ancestors are also using you to remind us that we must keep our traditions intact while we are in this new land. We must be careful not to neglect our traditions and culture which keep us grounded in life. We'll have to get started right away. I will discuss it with the council and then we'll let you know when it is time for your training to begin."

Dumisai heard the words being spoken but his thoughts were still trained on Baba Kenje's earlier comments.

"Baba, when it's time for me to leave, how long will I have to be gone?" he questioned, attempting to show that he could be brave in the face of the unknown.

"Ultimately, Dumisai, you came to earth to fulfill your destiny," Baba Kenje asserted, "and that, my boy, can take most people several lifetimes to accomplish. You, however, have been chosen to do something very important which must be completed in this lifetime. I'm afraid that this *is* your life's work, son. Your place is not here with us, but out in the world. Now, that is not to say that you cannot return to visit from time to time, but you must accept what the Creator has ordained for you if you are to be successful in life."

Dumisai mulled over the words spoken by the elder. He knew deep down that Baba Kenje was correct; that this was what he was supposed to be doing. He could choose to do something different, yet that possibility was so far removed that it was not even an option. Baba Kenje saw that Dumisai was receptive and was pleased with the boy's display of maturity.

"Now Dumisai," he continued, "we must prepare you for what lies ahead. Lest we abandon all that we know to be proper, let us bring this matter before the council. Together we will help you plan your journey away from us."

The old woman stepped forward, inserting her hunched body directly in front of Dumisai as she finally made preparation to speak, wanting to make sure that the boy fully understood what had been communicated. "How you do what must be done, boy, will depend on your understanding of the workings of this world and the other." Her voice was dry and creaky as the words slowly escaped through her lips, but Dumisai was careful not to miss a single syllable. "Yes, one day soon you will have to leave us, but you must not be afraid of what awaits you. The Creator has apportioned all things according to the divine plan. Your training will help you to know what is required of you. It is then that you will be able to fulfill your destiny, eh?"

"How will I know if my training has been successful?" Dumisai asked, careful not to speak out of turn while addressing the elderly woman.

"You will know," Manzalele replied. "One always knows. Still, success can be measured in different ways, eh? Your success will depend on your ability to understand and apply what you learn along the way."

Satisfied that Dumisai sufficiently understood what was required of him, Baba Kenje moved to wrap up the discussion. "It will be difficult seeing you depart from us, Dumisai, but no one can keep you from your appointed date with destiny, son. We may not be able to answer all of your questions at this time, but that which we cannot answer will surely be revealed at the appropriate time in the future. I will see that the council meets tonight and that your parents are properly informed of what must be done."

Having provided Dumisai with an explanation that he felt should be adequate, Baba Kenje looked to Manzalele who then placed her hand upon the top of the boy's head and whispered some words. Dumisai could not make out the words, but her gentle touch was reassuring and comforting, and he knew that she was placing a protection around him. The elders then left the boy and headed back toward the main village circle. All that was left for them to do now was to inform the other council members of the emergency meeting that would be needed to discuss Dumisai's future.

4: Separation

Dumisai ran as fast as his feet would carry him, frantically trying to out-distance the pursuing creature. He cast a quick glance over his shoulder to see how close the thing had gotten. Unfortunately, it was too dark to see much of anything, and he couldn't risk slowing down to check whether it was still behind him or not. He continued running, terrified that the creature might still be on his heels. In his haste, he didn't bother trying to dodge anything that could be moved aside. Luckily, there was sufficient light reflected by the moon to illuminate the trail in front of him, allowing him to at least avoid the forest trees as he ran. He clutched his side as the painful stitch of fatigue became impossible to ignore. It felt like he had been running for hours and he knew he could not keep up the pace for much longer. Finally, he slowed from sheer exhaustion while simultaneously checking frantically behind himself. There was nothing there. Dumisai breathed a sigh of relief. Maybe it was safe to rest for just a moment. He stopped and looked around cautiously as he bent over in an attempt to fill his lungs with adequate breaths of air. There was still no sign of the creature. Dumisai wondered if he was finally safe, using the brief respite to look around in a desperate attempt to figure out exactly where he was. He could see the edge of the forest not too far ahead. Just beyond the clearing, he spotted a hut through the trees. If he hurried, he could make a run to the dwelling for safety. Though still not yet rested, he was sure that his escape depended on getting out of the forest and into the safety of the hut. As he pushed forward, he began to recognize some of the surroundings. The familiarity was encouraging. Dumisai picked up his pace in an attempt to make it out of the woods. There was no mistake; somehow he had made it back to his home. The realization made him more determined than ever to reach the safety of his hut. Only a few more yards and he would be able to rest. He approached the door trying desperately to get inside. As he pushed it open, he saw a swirling group of lights quickly coalesce into a shadowy, wraith-like figure standing in the doorway and blocking his path. Dumisai panicked as his body became stiff with fear. The thing paused momentarily as if waiting to see the boy's reaction. It had no face, yet appeared to enjoy watching Dumisai's terrified surprise. Then suddenly, the creature began to transform, morphing into an airy specter-like whorl, sucking the light out of the world surrounding Dumisai and leaving him engulfed in total darkness. Dumisai tried to scream but no sounds came...

Dumisai bolted upright in bed with his fists clenched, ready to defend himself. The nightmare had wrested him out of his troubled sleep, leaving him gasping for air. The light shining through his window seemed brighter than normal which contributed to his disoriented state. It took several moments for him to get his bearings before realizing that he was still at home. It had simply been another nightmare, yet it had seemed so real. He still didn't have any idea what any of it meant, but he did remember more details than with his previous experiences. He replayed the specifics that he was able to recall over in his head, attempting to make some sense out of the events. It was no use—nothing in his life seemed to have any connection to the occurrences in the nightmare. He let out a sigh of frustration as he lay back down in bed, hoping to return to the sleep that had been abruptly interrupted. After lying awake for several minutes, Dumisai abandoned any hope of going back to sleep. It was past the time that he would normally be up and about anyway. He climbed out of bed slowly, allowing his body an opportunity to recover from his lethargy.

As Dumisai washed the morning sleep out of his eyes, he detected the savory smell of breakfast which was quickly filling the air throughout the dwelling. The tempting aroma teasingly prodded at him to speed his progress along. He was just finishing washing up when the sound of voices just beyond the hut's entrance caught his attention. The words were loud and distracting, leading Dumisai to wonder who was responsible for the disturbance as he peered through the window opening of the hut. The culprit was Baba Kenje as well as another man with whom Dumisai was only slightly familiar. The two men were speaking to his father and obviously unconcerned about the reach of their voices extending beyond the ears of their intended audience. Dumisai watched the exchange briefly and could see that his father was engaged in the discussion even though his involvement was mostly limited to listening and nodding in agreement.

"Dumisai?!!" Bento finally called to his son. "Dumisai!! I need you out here."

Dumisai pushed through the door to the attention of the three waiting men.

"Dumisai," Bento continued, "you know Baba Kenje and Sasombo. They've come to inform you that you'll be leaving today for your *Mukanda* initiation. Your mother has already prepared breakfast. After you finish eating, you will go with them to become a man. Go inside now and see if your mother needs any help preparing the table."

"Yes sir," Dumisai answered respectfully.

Malaika was listening just inside the entrance way to the hut. She hugged her son tightly as he re-entered the dwelling. The pride she felt toward him because he was about to leave to become a man had not quelled her motherly concern for his well-being while he was going to be away. She lovingly led Dumisai to the kitchen table while trying to keep her emotions in check. As she prepared his plate, she wiped a tear from her cheek but was careful not to allow her son to see that she had been crying. Dumisai appreciated the special breakfast that she had prepared for him. He ate slowly, using the opportunity to spend some quality time with his mother before standing to excuse himself from the table. Almost as if on cue, he heard his father speaking to some men who were approaching outside. Dumisai anxiously exited through the door, anticipating that the time for his departure had arrived. What appeared to be a man dressed in ceremonial garments and wearing a mask met Dumisai as he stepped outside, abruptly halting the boy's forward progress. Dumisai immediately recognized the character as an ancestor spirit known as an *Akishi*. He knew that the ancestors always made their presence known during important ceremonies and rituals by possessing the body of some individual for the purpose of imparting specific instructions to the people. Not far behind the ancestor were Sasombo and Baba Kenje. The *Akishi* looked at Dumisai curiously as if it was attempting to verify that it had found a suitable candidate for the initiation process. Sasombo quickly approached Dumisai who was still standing motionless before the *Akishi*, and rubbed an ointment of oil and clay over his body. After he was done, the two men followed the ancestor away from the village while escorting Dumisai to a secluded location.

The initiation camp was marked off by strategically placed pegs and blood-laced sticks intended to ward off bad spirits and uninitiated intruders. By the entrance stood another masked being. Its mask was tall with something in the shape of an antelope horn jutting skyward. Dumisai recognized it as the ancestral spirit *Chikunza*—the guardian of the initiation encampment. Its painted body was clothed in a grass skirt and swayed back and forth, moving in a slow dance-like motion while waving a sword in its right hand. Dumisai was careful not to lose cognizance of his escorts, but he was enthralled as he watched the *Chikunza* execute the warrior dance just outside the entrance to the camp.

Once inside, Dumisai's attention shifted to the layout of the encampment which he knew was going to serve as his new home for the duration of the *Mukanda* initiation process. Sasombo appeared to be in charge of the camp enclosure. Dumisai noticed how everyone, even Baba Kenje, got their direction from him. Sasombo insisted on maintaining a strict discipline within the enclosure and each of the camp attendants seemed obliged to enforce his wishes. His first order of business would be to circumcise Dumisai, which was an act of purification that all men had to endure. Sasombo had some of the men lead Dumisai to a previously prepared spot in order to perform the ritual exercise. Other attendants played drums while Sasombo began his surgical procedure with a razor. Dumisai lay on his back, determined not to cry out as Sasombo cut the necessary incisions in his flesh. After a seeming eternity, the ordeal was finally over. Sasombo treated the cuts with an antiseptic made of paste to help the wound heal. The healing process usually took up to two weeks, which allowed a good amount of time for the camp attendants to impart valuable lessons on becoming a man. Sasombo and the other men used the time to provide the necessary instructions on discipline and adult life. Dumisai was only allowed to speak when given explicit permission by one of the attendants and sometimes had to sit for hours without moving. His training also consisted of important cultural traditions which included mask-making and performing traditional songs and dance. He was expected to perfect all of what he was taught.

The days went by slowly at first due to the strict regimen, but Dumisai did not fret. He knew that he was learning invaluable lessons which would be necessary for his transition to manhood. After two and a half weeks, the cuts from the circumcision procedure were completely healed. Dumisai was now ready to resume the purification process. Sasombo and the other men led Dumisai to a location along the river which was in close proximity to the village. To Dumisai's surprise, the entire village was waiting when he arrived. They were just close enough to watch the event without interfering as he prepared to enter the water. He could see his parents, as well as the other adults looking on proudly but Dumisai maintained his demeanor. The experience in the secluded camp had exacted firm disciplinary results. Malaika waved excitedly, trying to get her son's attention but Dumisai remained focused. He stepped into the river nearly oblivious to his surroundings, focusing solely on the task in front of him. Slowly and deliberately, he bathed himself according to the instructions he had been given. Once finished, he was led back to the encampment, his mood still as solemn as when he had first arrived at the river.

An elder attendant named Malekazi who was responsible for dispensing instructions during the afternoon sessions wanted to ensure that Dumisai was reminded of his obligations. He sat cross-legged across from Dumisai, accompanied by a younger man named T'Chomba.

"You must not disclose any of what you have been taught, Dumisai," Malekazi explained. "The instructions you have been given are for you alone. Is that clear?"

"Yes sir."

"Each initiate receives what he needs. But we know about you Dumisai. Everyone here knows that you are the one that Niangi was speaking about. Because of that, there will be some special training for you that is not intended for other *Tundanji*."

"That's right, Dumisai," added T'Chomba, "what Malekazi is saying is true. There is a lot that you still have to learn, but much of it we cannot teach you. Some things are beyond the reach of the average person."

Dumisai continued listening to the men without interrupting. He knew he would be prompted to speak if a response was required. The men sometimes covered the same information which had been given on previous occasions but he was grateful for the repetition because it assisted his memorization of the lessons.

After the day's instruction was complete, Dumisai was looking forward to sleeping on his newly prepared pallet. Since the purification bath, he was no longer required to sleep between the pegs outlining his spot on the ground, but was allowed instead to sleep using a mat and blanket. Once he laid down, he found it ironic that the more comfortable bedding did not help him to fall asleep. Dumisai was restless throughout the evening, drifting in and out of sleep while constantly changing positions in an attempt to get comfortable. By midnight, he finally succumbed to sleep and was oblivious to the waking world. Within minutes, his dream-induced subconscious was overtaken by a recurring familiar scene. His awareness was immediately drawn into the little hut that sat in the middle of a forest clearing.

Dumisai peeked through a crack in the door, desperately trying to maintain his stealth as he spied on the activity in the other room. The sight in front of him froze him in absolute horror. The bodies of his mother, father, and sister all lay in a puddle of blood; their limbs separated from their bodies. The faceless creature stood over its victims as if it was silently celebrating a job well-done. Dumisai felt a shiver run up his spine. He knew he would have to flee if he was to avoid the fate suffered by the rest of his family. As he started to back away, he heard voices from outside the hut quickly approaching. His first instinct was to scream out to the approaching people for help, but before he could even open his mouth he saw the group of men that were approaching. They were dressed in strange garments and carried rifles which were flung over their shoulder. Dumisai was perplexed by the appearance of the men. Their skin was white and they spoke a strange language, frequently interspersing their words with bouts of laughter. He quickly dashed behind the first basket he could find to avoid detection. Luckily, the men were preoccupied with each other when they entered the hut and did not notice him as they passed directly into the room with his murdered family. Dumisai peeked from behind his hiding place in an attempt to see what the men were doing. The shadowy figure was still present but it was no longer the faceless creature that he had seen standing over his family. It had changed into a man like the others. Dumisai listened intently, hoping to decipher some information from their strange sounding conversation, but he could not understand anything except an occasional word here and there. For some reason the words "Congo" and "Katanga" sounded familiar to him. He did not know what the words meant, yet they gave him a feeling of Déjà vu. "Leopold...," one of the men called out to his comrades. The sound of the name nearly panicked Dumisai. He quickly pulled another item in front of his body, attempting to bolster his hiding place. When he looked up again, one of the men was standing directly over him, smiling triumphantly as he menacingly pointed his machete toward the boy. Dumisai was paralyzed with fear. The man seemed to enjoy seeing the terror in the boy's eyes. He slowly lowered his machete, placing the edge of the blade against Dumisai's chest as if toying with him. The shirt offered little resistance as the blade sliced cleanly through it while carving an "X" across Dumisai's heart. Blood trickled down Dumisai's shirt, staining his clothing a bright and vibrant red.

"Nooo...!" Dumisai screamed while jumping up into a seated position. He stared blankly into the star-filled night as he recalled the violence of the nightmare. The image of the slain people in the dream was etched firmly into his memory. Dumisai exhaled a sigh of relief upon realizing that it was only a dream, but was beginning to become concerned by the violent nature of the hauntings. He was convinced that he should talk to an elder to see if someone could help him sort out the meaning. One of the elders should be able to tell him if some message was being communicated or if the dream portended some potential threat, especially if he was experiencing something that went beyond the boundaries of a simple nightmare. Unfortunately, the answer would have to wait until morning because the surrounding darkness signaled that it was still the middle of the night.

Dumisai tried desperately to forget about the nightmare. He trained his thoughts instead on the events that had led to his discovery of the *Gift* as he prepared to go back to sleep. Within minutes his thoughts were completely focused on the more pleasant memory. As he shifted his body in an attempt to get comfortable on the pallet, he felt something sticky against his skin. Dumisai poked at the spot gingerly, curious to why his shirt was wet and clinging to his belly. Slowly, he looked down, afraid of what he might discover. His shirt was soaked red with blood. He hurriedly ripped it open, revealing a fresh flesh wound in the shape of an "X" on his chest. Upon seeing the actual wound, Dumisai walked anxiously over to the camp attendants' hut. No one was up, and their huts were quiet except for a soft snore that trailed though the night air. After briefly contemplating whether to alert the attendants, he thought better of waking the men and instead returned to his mat determined to maintain his courage. Suddenly, a rustling noise in the nearby bushes startled him again. He looked around nervously, searching for the source of the noise. He knew it would be next to impossible to go to sleep now. He was too afraid to move except for the sudden jerk of his head turning to get a glimpse of anything making a noise around him.

Thud!

The sudden noise frightened Dumisai, causing him to whirl back around quickly to his front. Standing directly beyond his outstretched feet was the *Chikunza*.

"COME," the ancestor instructed.

Dumisai sat momentarily frozen in his seat, mesmerized by the ancestor. After slowly summoning his courage, he stood and followed the *Chikunza* through the wooded area. They plodded through the dark forest until eventually reaching the river. Dumisai recognized the location as the spot where he had taken his purification bath. Upon reaching the shore, the *Chikunza* continued walking, trudging directly into the river without pause. Dumisai hesitated briefly before following. The ancestor continued its march into the river until its head was completely submerged. As the water reached up to Dumisai's chest, he dipped his head beneath the surface hoping to maintain his close proximity to the *Chikunza*. The nighttime darkness made it impossible to see anything in the water. Dumisai reached out, feeling around for the ancestor without success. Finally, he began swimming just below the surface, hoping to locate his guide. He came up briefly to take a deep breath and then returned to his underwater search. He swam deeper this time, aware that he may soon reach the bottom of the river. As he descended further, the floor of the riverbed began to come into view. Dumisai noticed that the water appeared to be getting brighter despite the nighttime darkness, as if he was swimming towards the surface during daylight rather than deeper into its murky depths. He continued his effortless descent, almost as if his body was being pulled in a current. He noticed that the deeper he went, the more illumined the water became. After arriving at the bottom of the river, he reached out for the white, clay soil lining the riverbed, expecting it to stop his descent, but instead his hand shot through the water's surface. His head also quickly emerged from the water, allowing him to inhale deeply in order to fill his lungs with oxygen before swimming to the shore.

As he climbed up on the riverbank with his body still dripping wet, Dumisai slowly took in the beautiful view of the scenery as he attempted to get his bearings. He glanced briefly at the sky, amazed at how bright and clear the day was. The sun was shining high at mid-day as if intentionally showcasing the total effulgence of its power. Dumisai didn't even dwell on fact that the night had suddenly become day, but instead focused on where he was at. The surrounding area appeared to be completely foreign. He searched anxiously, looking around for some recognizable clue to where his journey had taken him. He was sure that there was very little territory near the village that he was not intimately familiar with, yet this location was completely foreign to him. Even the river looked different. It was much wider than he remembered and lined with tropical plants.

Dumisai continued exploring. He pushed through the thick of the trees and shrubs of the forest, noticing vibrant green foliage which he had never seen before. A loud growl off in the distance temporarily immobilized him with fear. Slowly, he peered from behind the large leaves of a viney bush to investigate the noise. A large black panther, its muscles glistening against the bright rays of the sun, was stalking its prey. Dumisai moved away cautiously as he surveyed the trees around him. A colorful macaw caught his attention from a nearby tree branch. Dumisai slowly began to realize that the animals he was observing were not native to the Oklahoma that he was familiar with. His suspicion was confirmed by the loud screeches of two spider monkeys chasing each other through the treetops overhead. Dumisai didn't know where the *Chikunza* had taken him but he was sure that he was no longer anywhere near his village. Far off in the distance he thought he could hear the faint sound of drums. He stopped and strained his ears, attempting to determine which direction the drumming was coming from. He began moving ahead in the chosen direction, passing different animals along the way. The animals didn't pay him any attention and Dumisai was content to leave it that way. His immediate concern was to acquaint himself with the unfamiliar surroundings of the mysterious forest so that he could determine where he was.

Dumisai walked for nearly twenty minutes before finally approaching the edge of a clearing. Just beyond the trees he saw a crowd of onlookers encircling a group of drummers that were playing for several dancers. The drumming was loud and infectious, enticing the village spectators to actively participate in the apparent celebration. He could hear the assembly as they began chanting in unison and did not want to intrude. Dumisai stopped momentarily upon recognizing the phrase that they were repeating. *"CHIN-GEL-YEN-GEL-YE".* He was vaguely familiar with the term which seemed to stir something deep within his being, but he did not stop to dwell on the meaning of the obscure word. He still needed to speak to someone in order to find out where his journey had led him but was unsure how to gain the group's attention without disrupting the occasion. He continued watching from a distance as the frenetic pace of the drumbeat continued to hold sway over the dancers, commanding them to move as they flounced energetically to the driving rhythm. It seemed that the entire village must have been in attendance at the event and they were adorned with some of their most colorful and fashionable attire. Slowly, Dumisai began to make his way around the edge of the clearing without leaving the confines of the forest while searching for the best location to enter without drawing too much attention to himself. Once he reached a spot where the majority of the people had their backs to him, he summoned enough courage to enter. The moment he stepped into the village clearing the drumming suddenly stopped. He felt a strange, tingly sensation pass through his body, leaving him feeling slightly dizzy for a few moments. He tried clearing his head, unsure of what had happened while simultaneously noticing that the entire village had apparently emptied. Everyone was suddenly gone along with their musical instruments. It was as if they had all vanished into thin air. Dumisai looked around slowly, unsure what had happened to all the people. He began investigating the village, hoping to find some evidence of the celebration that he had just witnessed.

As he walked, Dumisai noticed how the huts appeared to be suffering from years of neglect and a general lack of attention. Most were in desperate need of repair. In fact, everything looked rundown. Perhaps he simply hadn't noticed before because his attention had been so focused on the drumming and dancing, but he still couldn't get past the fact that the village atmosphere had a strange, unearthly feel to it. Dumisai began looking in the huts, desperate to find anyone who might possibly still be around. He was convinced that he had not imagined the earlier celebration and began running from hut to hut, but was still unable to find anyone. Not a single person was around. Frustrated and confused, he finally abandoned his search and returned to the spot where he thought he had seen the dancers. He sat on the ground for a moment to catch his breath and clear his head. Burying his face in his hands, he exhaled a frustrated sigh. Finally, in a moment of resignation, he decided to retrace his steps back through the woods.

As he began climbing to his feet, Dumisai noticed a bald-headed, muscular man, who appeared to be in his mid-forties and was dressed in white, standing several feet in front of him. Dumisai was surprised by the sudden arrival of the man who seemed to have appeared out of nowhere. He noticed that the bald man had a diamond-shaped pendant with triangles on each corner attached to his forehead, and was accompanied by many other men and women. Looking around slowly, Dumisai could see that he was completely surrounded by people. They were all dressed in flowing white garments. Many of the women wore white head wraps. Both the men and women looked as though they were preparing for ritual. Dumisai finished standing up slowly, unsure of what was happening.

"Dumisai," the bald gentleman in front said with a thick African accent, **"do not be afraid."**

"Huh?" a confused Dumisai half mumbled in bewilderment, "how do you know my name?"

"We know all about you, Dumisai. We know who you are and we know your ancestral lineage."

The man's voice sounded hollow and distant yet distinctly baritone.

"Many of whom that you now see here before you came through that lineage," the man continued. **"Have you not yet figured out where you are, Dumisai?"**

"No… sir," he responded nervously.

"HA, HA. ISN'T IT OBVIOUS, SON? YOU HAVE ENTERED THE LAND OF THE DEAD!"

"What…? I don't understand."

"DUMISAI, WE ARE YOUR ANCESTORS. IN FACT, MANY OF US HAVE A DIRECT CONNECTION TO YOU THROUGH YOUR BLOODLINE. LOOK AROUND—WHO KNOWS, HA HA— YOU MIGHT JUST SEE SOMEONE YOU KNOW."

Dumisai briefly scanned the faces in the crowd.

"IT'S ALRIGHT, SON," a tall, regal-looking woman voiced encouragingly. "WE ARE ALL FAMILY HERE."

"WE ARE INDEED," the bald man continued. "NOW LET ME TELL YOU: IT IS NO ACCIDENT THAT YOU ARE HERE, DUMISAI. THIS IS AN ESSENTIAL PART OF YOUR MANHOOD TRAINING. WE BROUGHT YOU HERE SO THAT WE MAY TRANSMIT TO YOU THE ANCESTRAL WISDOM OF OUR PEOPLE. NOW, TELL ME SOMETHING: AFTER HAVING HAD THIS EXPERIENCE, CAN YOU NOT SAY THAT WE ARE REAL?"

"Yes… I guess."

"YOU GUESS? DO YOU NOT TRUST YOUR OWN EYES?"

"Yes sir… I do."

"THEN WHAT IS THERE TO GUESS ABOUT?"

"I… don't know, sir."

"HA HA HAH—YOU ARE TRYING TOO HARD TO FORCE THINGS TO MAKE SENSE, DUMISAI. SOMETIMES YOU JUST HAVE TO TRUST WHAT HAS BEEN REVEALED TO YOU."

"Yes… I know."

"VERY GOOD, DUMISAI! AND NOW, SINCE YOU KNOW THAT WE ARE REAL, YOU HAVE NO REASON TO DOUBT THAT WE ARE ALWAYS WITH YOU. ISN'T THAT SO?"

"Yes sir."

"GOOD—WE ALWAYS KNEW YOU WERE THE ONE FOR THIS TIME, DUMISAI. EVEN BEFORE YOU WERE FORMED IN YOUR MOTHER'S WOMB, WE HAVE KNOWN YOU."

Dumisai remained silent, still visibly uncomfortable.

"**A FITTING VESSEL THROUGH WHICH THE CREATOR CAN COME INTO THE WORLD, DON'T YOU ALL AGREE?**" the man asked rhetorically while directing his attention to the gathering of ancestors assembled in the clearing.

"**YES,**" came the response in a disconcerted cacophony of murmurs.

"**SO, YOU SEE, DUMISAI,**" the bald gentleman continued, again focusing his attention on the boy, "**WE ARE HERE FOR YOU. ALL THAT YOU SEE BEFORE YOU, AND EVEN MANY THOUSANDS MORE WHO HAVE 'DIED', ARE HERE TO HELP YOU. WHEN YOU NEED US, WE WILL BE THERE. WE MAY NOT HAVE A BODY TO MOVE ABOUT THE PHYSICAL WORLD, BUT WE WILL ALWAYS MAKE OUR PRESENCE KNOWN. DO YOU UNDERSTAND THAT?**"

"Yes sir."

"**GOOD, IT IS IMPORTANT THAT YOU UNDERSTAND THESE THINGS.**"

The man's gentle tone helped Dumisai to relax a little.

"**DUMISAI, YOU HAVE A GREAT WORK TO DO IN THIS LIFETIME—DO IT WITH DIGNITY AND HONOR. IN SO DOING YOU WILL HONOR US. CAN YOU DO THAT, SON?**"

"Yes sir."

"**GOOD. IN YOUR SHORT YEARS, YOU HAVE LEARNED MUCH. YOU MUST NEVER STOP DOING SO. AS LONG AS YOU ARE OPEN TO LEARNING AND USING WHAT YOU HAVE LEARNED FOR GOOD, THE CREATOR WILL BE ABLE TO USE YOU. YOU ARE LIVING IN A WORLD THAT IS IN NEED OF GUIDANCE, BUT BEFORE YOU CAN GUIDE OTHERS OUT OF THE DARKNESS OF THIS WORLD, PEOPLE MUST BE ABLE TO SEE THE LIGHT THAT SHINES WITHIN YOU.**" The man paused in order to focus Dumisai's attention. "**IT MATTERS NOT THAT YOU HAVEN'T BEEN CORRUPTED BY THE WAYS OF THIS WORLD, DUMISAI. YOU WILL STILL BE TESTED IN THIS LIFE. BUT THAT IS AS IT SHOULD BE BECAUSE THAT IS THE ONLY PATH TO SPIRITUAL POWER. SO, DO NOT GIVE**

IN TO TEMPTATION WHEN IT COMES—BUT HOLD ON TO WHAT IS RIGHT."

"Yes sir, I will."

"GOOD—AND REMEMBER, DUMISAI, GOD IS WITH YOU BUT YOU CANNOT SINGLE-HANDEDLY SAVE THE BILLIONS OF LOST SOULS OUT IN THE WORLD. YOU CAN ONLY SAVE YOURSELF. ONCE YOU SAVE YOURSELF, THEN THROUGH YOU OTHERS WILL ALSO BE SAVED. AS LONG AS YOU MAKE SURE THAT YOUR ACTIONS ARE IN HARMONY WITH GOD'S LAW, YOU WILL BLESS THOSE THAT YOU COME IN CONTACT WITH. AND BLESS THEM YOU WILL, HA HA! THAT IS GOD'S LOVE IN ACTION AND IT SHALL SPREAD ACROSS THE LAND INFLUENCING MILLIONS. THIS IS WHAT YOU HAVE BEEN CALLED BY GOD TO DO."

The man smiled wide as he finished inspecting Dumisai.

"SO, DUMISAI, DO YOU UNDERSTAND ALL THAT WE HAVE SHARED WITH YOU?"

"Yes sir."

"GOOD—HA HA! THEN OUR WORK IS DONE FOR NOW. REMEMBER DUMISAI, WE ARE WITH YOU, ALWAYS!"

Dumisai could tell that man's words were a signal that the time had come for the gathering to disperse. Slowly, each of the ancestors began to disappear one by one, until only the man who had been speaking and the tall lady remained. The man nodded to Dumisai with a slight smile and then vanished. The lady extended her hands out to the boy, grasping his firmly but gently.

"MY HUSBAND, NIANGI, IS RIGHT, YOU KNOW," she said softly, her eyes staring directly into his. "WE ARE ALL SO PROUD OF YOU." Then she too was gone.

"Wait!"

His appeal was in vain as he anxiously searched around the clearing, disappointed that he had not been given the opportunity to find out more about her.

The sun, along with the light it had ushered in, suddenly disappeared. Dumisai found himself staring up into the night sky, unable to comprehend the sudden departure of daylight. Water rushed past his feet and up the side of his body which lay on the ground, making its way all the way to his head. A small portion of the cold liquid entered his left ear, causing him to sit up abruptly. As he looked around, he recognized the spot along the river where the *Akishi* had initially led him into the water. Even though it was still dark, he drew some comfort from the fact that at least he knew where he was. Slowly, he climbed to his feet, his soaked clothes still dripping with water. He walked away from the edge of the river where the water had washed up onto his body while noticing that the sun was just beneath the horizon and a new day was about to break. The *Chikunza* was nowhere to be found. Dumisai shrugged, unsure whether he had just awakened from a lucid dream. Eyeing the trail that led to the river, he turned to begin his trek back through the woods to the initiation camp.

5: The Apprentice

Dumisai pushed through the underbrush that was partially obstructing the wooded trail as the light of a new day threatened to overtake the horizon. He expected to reach the initiation camp by sunrise even though he was not consciously keeping track of the time. With his thoughts still focused on the events of the previous night, he did not notice the presence of someone walking towards him until they were standing almost directly in front of him. The sudden realization startled Dumisai, causing him to jump back as he attempted to ascertain the identity of the person causing his alarm. Standing there staring at him was Ol' Manzalele. The old woman's presence alone was enough to fill the boy with fear. He knew immediately that running into her was more than a simple coincidence. As he looked into her pale, expressionless face, he could feel the penetrating stare of her pink eyes peering into his as if they were attempting to pierce all the way through to his soul. After what seemed like an eternity to the frightened boy, the old woman broke the long silence.

"Come with me," she stated firmly.

"B-But… the camp," he stuttered.

"The next stage of your training will be my responsibility," she informed him before turning in the direction from which she had come. She was completely devoid of emotion. Dumisai obeyed, his previous thoughts now totally obliterated. The thought of disobeying an elder was foreign to him, yet because he was so terrified of the old woman, he actually considered running off into the woods. Ultimately though, it was that same fear that made him stay put. With her presence demanding obedience, Dumisai followed as she began walking back to her destination. He purposely walked at a slower pace in order to lag a little behind so as to avoid having to engage in any conversation with the woman. Her gait was also slow and labored as she relied heavily upon her walking stick to help her get around, yet her movements were very deliberate and determined. She never bothered to check behind her to verify whether the boy was following or not. Dumisai dared not do anything else but follow. He had heard stories about the woman's *powers* and did not want to risk being on the receiving end of anything that wasn't intended as a blessing. After what seemed like a long walk, they arrived at the old woman's dwelling located on the opposite end of the village.

"You have been chosen," the woman blurted out in a dry, hoarse voice while turning to face the boy who was standing just beyond the entrance to her hut. Dumisai wasn't sure if her words were intended as a statement or as a question so he decided that the safest thing to do was to just keep quiet.

"You have the *Gift*, but you must learn to use it, eh? Only then will you be able to make the difference that is required of you," she continued, her tone almost chastising as she spoke. "Do not be afraid, boy," she added sensing Dumisai's uneasiness, "I am here to help you. There is nothing that you need fear from me as long as you use what has been given to you for good." She paused momentarily, releasing a heavy breath through her nostrils and causing Dumisai to wonder whether she needed to catch her breath or was simply sighing. "The ancestors have instructed me to teach you in the full use of your *power*. I am a diviner... a spiritual healer—what we used to call '*N'ganga*' back in the home country. That means that I have learned the use of our secret wisdom, but unlike you I do not possess the *Gift*. Still, there is much that I can teach you if you are willing to learn, eh?"

Dumisai found some comfort listening to the old woman speak and was able to relax a little. He was surprised to hear her talk so much since he had rarely heard her say much of anything prior to this occasion. "I know that I still have a lot to learn, ma'am," Dumisai responded shyly and unsure about anything except being agreeable, "and I would appreciate all that you can teach me."

"Good. Let us get started then."

Manzalele entered into her dwelling while motioning for Dumisai to follow. The boy had to summon his courage again before entering into the hut. Once inside, he saw that different items were spread all around the living area. He quickly surveyed the dimly lit room attempting to file away as many details as possible into his memory. He noticed several gourds and clay pots, as well as a few flat divination baskets. Many of the artifacts were placed in what appeared to be strategic locations around the hut. Contained within some of the clay pots was a liquid substance that could possibly have been water. The poor lighting made it difficult to determine exactly what the liquid was but Dumisai guessed that it was probably responsible for the dank and musty odor infesting his nostrils as he walked slowly through the hut. Before he could finish his survey, the woman continued through to the other side of the dwelling exiting into another room.

As Dumisai turned to follow Manzalele, his eyes came across a separate area of the hut. At first, he almost didn't notice it in the dim lighting because the entrance had been partially covered in an apparent attempt at sectioning it off from the rest of the hut. There was something about the room however, that seemed to tug at his imagination, causing him to strain his eyes as he attempted to probe the room's obscure darkness in search of any secrets that it might be willing to reveal. Peering into the dark space, he was convinced that something important must be hidden within it, and felt that it was enticing him to come inside. The temptation to enter was strong, yet Dumisai hesitated. He wasn't sure if his diffidence was out of respect for the old woman's privacy or if something else was giving him reason to pause. Still, the urge to explore the room continued to build before finally becoming too much to resist, causing Dumisai to ignore any reluctance he held toward entering. As he slowly poked his head into the doorway, the *klang* of a falling pot from the kitchen area abruptly shocked him back to his senses. Dumisai instantly directed his attention back to the old woman and began moving quickly in her direction to avoid being left alone in any part of the hut any longer. Realizing that she had disappeared into another section of the hut, Dumisai picked up his pace in order to catch up to her. Once he reached the entrance to the room where she was standing, he was pleasantly surprised to find it slightly illuminated by a candle which Manzalele was in the process of placing onto a nearby table.

"Do not allow yourself to become so easily distracted, Dumisai," the old woman said just as he entered. She never looked up when she spoke, as if she had anticipated the exact moment of his arrival.

"I'm sorry," Dumisai apologized, realizing that the woman had caught him snooping. "It won't happen again."

She turned and looked directly into his eyes. "If the spirit is weak, one could leave himself open to attack by psychic forces."

The forcefulness of the statement surprised Dumisai.

"Ma'am?"

"If your spiritual defenses are weak, then you will be vulnerable to attack. All one has to do is manipulate energy in such a way that it can be used against you."

"I don't understand...," Dumisai admitted.

"Your thoughts, boy," the woman explained, "they are the gateway to your spirit."

"Yes... ma'am...," Dumisai acknowledged, though he was still unsure what had prompted the statement.

"What I want you to understand, Dumisai, is that the thoughts that constitute your mind can place you at risk if they are not based on truth."

Dumisai stopped his forward progress in order to devote his full attention to the woman's assertion.

"Once you accept a thought into your mind," she continued, "it affects your energy—your life force."

Dumisai was intrigued. "Any thought...? What if the thought doesn't represent reality?"

"Dumisai, I'm speaking about energy. Ultimately, everything is energy, eh? Our thoughts, our emotions, psychic phenomena, even this table here—it is all energy—it's just that the energy has been manipulated into the reality that we experience daily. In the same way, your thoughts can be used to manipulate you."

"But doesn't a thought only have power if you believe in it?" he asked, attempting to reason out the lesson that Manzalele had presented.

"No, boy—I'm telling you that energy can be manipulated for good or bad results depending on the intention behind it. It's no different than electricity. What you choose to believe or not believe can only protect you to a point. What you need to do is make sure that you are always prepared to guard your thoughts!"

"Yes, ma'am."

By now, Dumisai was absorbed in Manzalele's instruction, recalling how the wisdom of the woman's words reminded him of his grandmother's lessons.

"Remember, Dumisai, you were chosen because the ancestors were able to see the light that shines within your spirit. But that same light can also be spotted by negative forces that may wish to do you harm. Never forget that you have the potential to be a major force for good in the world. But also know that whenever great power for good is invoked, certain forces will always try to stop it. This is what you must understand."

"Yes ma'am. I'm willing to do whatever I need to do in order to be successful."

"To be successful you will need to know the workings of the universe. When you understand the forces of nature, then you will see the truth that underlies all existence. It is this knowledge that will help you make the most of the *Gift*."

Dumisai realized that he was no longer afraid of the woman. A feeling of calm had come over him as she spoke, replacing his anxiety with an eagerness to learn all that she had to teach.

"We will begin by accessing that part of your spirit which is in touch with all things. It is possible to connect with the Creator that dwells within you if you know how. Have you ever had an answer to a problem that was vexing you be revealed even though you were not looking for it?"

"Yes," the boy replied.

"And how did you know that it was the answer that you needed to solve the problem?"

"I'm not really sure... I mean, I just knew, that's all."

"Of course. It is as I suspected."

"What do you mean?" Dumisai asked hesitantly.

"It is not expected that you will understand these things just yet, but you will in the proper time. Trust your intuition, boy. The ancestors knew what they were doing when they chose you to wield the power of the *Gift*. My goal is to help you cultivate that power so that you can call upon it at will, even at a moment's notice if necessary."

Dumisai watched as Manzalele retrieved a small pouch from the bag that she carried under her arm. She slowly emptied out its contents making a pile of *cowrie shells* on the table top. She then picked up the shells in both hands, holding them close to her mouth and whispering some words before tossing them down again. After inspecting the pattern made by the shells and their positions relative to each other, the woman looked to Dumisai and nodded with an expression that seemed to convey approval.

"The *Oracle* says that you will be tested mightily in this life's journey. If you are to be truly successful in life, you will have to confront your fears and overcome them. But don't fret, boy, nothing of value is ever given to one without them first proving that they are worthy to receive it, eh? So even though you have been chosen, your ability to use the *Gift* successfully will depend on whether or not you are able to slay the demons within you."

"Demons…?" Dumisai responded, recalling the nightmares that continue to plague him.

"I am speaking of those challenges in life which must be overcome before you are allowed to ascend to the higher powers of the spirit, boy. Like everyone, you have been placed here on earth by the Creator with a specific destiny. But in order to fulfill it, you must pass the tests of life, eh?"

"How will I know when I'm being tested?" Dumisai asked.

"You will know, Dumisai. Those things have a way of making themselves known. If you think back hard enough, you will discover that you have already had many such experiences during the course of your short life."

Dumisai thought about his recurring nightmares and wondered if this would be an appropriate time to bring up the subject. Manzalele sensed that the boy's thoughts had distracted him.

"No, not now boy," Manzalele interrupted, "there will be plenty of time to reflect on that later. Right now, we have other work to do, eh?"

Dumisai abruptly abandoned the search of his memory at the woman's command.

"What I have shown you here is called *divination*. It is a process by which you can talk to the Creator and receive divine counsel. Yet, it is only a substitute for knowing how to retrieve the answer to any question from within your own spirit."

Manzalele maneuvered her body in front of Dumisai as she looked him directly in the eye. "Is it not true that we are all made in the image and likeness of the Creator?"

"Yes, that is true."

"Then, if in truth, you are made in the image and likeness of the Creator who knows all things, it follows that you must have the same ability within you. The trick is in knowing how to access the knowledge. Until you have learned to do this with little effort, I will teach you how to use this system of divination so that you will have the means to find the answers to any of life's questions."

Dumisai listened closely as the woman explained the meaning behind the positioning of the *cowrie shells*. There was so much to learn and he was a willing student. He was enthralled by the idea of talking directly to God. Over the course of several days Manzalele reinforced what she had taught the boy by giving him an opportunity to practice what he had learned. She explained the secrets of the stars and how their energies affected activity on earth. Manzalele taught Dumisai the skill of going into deep trance in order to receive messages from various faculties of his spirit. He learned to manipulate herbs and stones so that he could affect the environment around him. Manzalele also equipped him with a small medicine bag that he was able to wear over his shoulder. The bag contained several items like those which the two of them had been working with, each neatly separated into an individual compartment. In addition to his assortment of herbs and charms, she supplied him with a canister for transporting a small quantity of water. "Never underestimate the importance of a drink of water, Dumisai," the woman told him, "it could mean the difference between life and death, eh?" She started him on a cleansing fast at the beginning of the second week to prepare him for the work to come. His diet was restricted to oranges, grapes and lots of water. Dumisai had never considered that there was so much to learn which he had not been exposed to before. He had always been content to simply commune with nature, but this woman was teaching him the secret to the mysteries of the universe itself.

After two full weeks under the direct tutelage of Manzalele, Dumisai was directed to the entrance by the dark room that had so captivated his attention upon his arrival at the hut. Standing by the doorway to the room, he was better able to see into it now, but it was still too dark to make out many of the details. As he looked into the shadowy room a chill ran through his body. Gone was the urge to enter that had once been so strong. Now, simply standing by the doorway was cause enough for uneasiness. He noticed a couple of *Makishi* masks along one of the walls next to several gourds that were connected together by a string rope. Underneath the gourds, a shrine erected on a small table caught his attention.

"What's in there?" Dumisai asked, the trepidation in his voice obvious.

"I cannot tell you what awaits you in there," the woman answered, "I *will* tell you that it is the place where I go when I want to travel between worlds. You can think of it as a kind of portal between the physical and supernatural realms if you like, but for me it is simply a sacred space—one that I have been using to perform rituals in since I arrived here. As a result, the energy in there is very charged."

She hesitated for a moment to catch her breath before continuing. Dumisai took advantage of the opportunity to inject a question. "If it is sacred, then why is it so spooky?"

"The sacred and the profane are but opposite ends of the same reality, eh? Separating the two is like trying to find exactly where hot ends and cold begins. The truth is: they both represent the same energy which manifests from a single source. How you relate to the energy determines your experience."

"Do I have to go in there?" Dumisai asked, the apprehension still recognizable in his voice.

"Yes boy, you must enter. It is in there that you must face your fears. What you find in there depends on how your spirit has been conditioned. But remember, a great reward awaits the one who can conquer his fears, overcome worldly distractions, and slay the demons that seek to beguile him. These are the challenges that we are confronted with daily. It's just that they often manifest as emotional and psychic trauma in our lives which then serves to distract us from achieving our divinity, and thus rob us of our greatest reward. Once you have completed this task, you will be ready for the next major stage of initiation."

Dumisai was afraid. He was convinced that the faceless creature from his nightmare would be waiting for him in the room. Since he still had no idea what the dreams meant, he felt defenseless and vulnerable. He knew the old woman was not going to give him an out, so he had no choice but to summon the courage needed to confront his fear. Taking one final glance at the old woman, as if he was looking for a bit of reassurance, Dumisai stepped through the doorway into the room. He could immediately feel the pulse of energy surging around him. The air was thick and caused the tiny hair follicles covering his skin to stand on end. He looked around the room anticipating some type of encounter but was unsure what form it might take. To his surprise, he did not see anything out of the ordinary. Slowly, his sense of adventure was beginning to replace his fear of being in the room. Dumisai turned toward the doorway to verify that the old woman was still there offering some comfort with her presence if he needed it, but she was gone. Her departure caused the boy's fear to resurface. The feeling of vulnerability returned as the realization set in that he was all alone. His mind began to race with a torrent of thoughts which were conspiring to heighten his fears.

Kla-shang!!!

A loud crashing noise which sounded like a glass object shattering against the back wall startled him, causing him to whirl around to see what had caused the ruckus. He could see from the pieces of glass scattered about the floor that it had once been a dish, but there was no way to tell where the object had come from. Before he could investigate further, Dumisai saw another dish hurling through the air and coming straight toward his head. He ducked instinctively, barely dodging the object. As he listened to it crash against the wall, he saw a large earthen pot rise from the floor as if it had a life of its own. Before the pot could reach Dumisai, he quickly ducked behind a desk table for cover.

"Stop it!" the boy shouted, his hands and arms folded over his head for protection.

Suddenly all was quiet again. After several moments of seeming peace, Dumisai peeked over the top of the table to make sure it was safe to come out from behind his cover. Over in the far corner of the room, he saw what looked like a person sitting, curled up on the floor with his head partially tucked between his knees. Looking closer, he could see that it was a man, probably in his early to mid forties. Dumisai came from behind the desk to get a closer look at the man who was still cowering in the corner. At first it was difficult to determine for certain if the man was attempting to protect himself from more objects which might be flying in his direction, or if he was simply cowering out of fear. As Dumisai got closer, the man looked up timidly and Dumisai could clearly see that the expression on the man's face was filled with terror. The man's terror-stricken expression caused Dumisai to completely forget his own fears.

"Hello…?" Dumisai asserted nervously, not sure of what he expected to hear in response. He slowly approached the frightened man, who was still cowering, until he was close enough to look directly into his eyes, hoping to identify some clue to the source of the man's anguish. The man's hopelessness seemed to draw Dumisai in as if the boy was looking through a window into another world at an immense amount of suffering. The pain and suffering seemed to surround him as he stood there transfixed, staring into the eyes of the man. Without realizing what had happened, he had somehow been transported right into the middle of several thousand people—men, women, and children—all of whom seemed to be experiencing an unbearable amount of pain. Dumisai was so taken by the scene that he completely lost touch with his own whereabouts. His presence among the people had gone unnoticed though, as no one paid any attention to him. Their voices filled the air around him with wailing and moans of agony. His heart lurched with anguish as he listened to the agonizing screams of the people. He did not recognize any single individual among them, yet he felt a connection to them which could not be denied. They appeared to be separated into groups, each of which was made up of many hundreds and sometimes even thousands of people. Most of the groups were of a predominant African ethnic origin or mixture, but a few were also of European and Native American ancestry. Each group seemed to have some identifiable set of characteristics that set it apart from the others.

Dumisai noticed how one group of people's clothing was ragged and torn. Many of the individuals making up this group of mostly adults were wearing clothes that were beyond repair and soaked with blood. Through the tattered clothing which dangled loosely from their bodies, Dumisai could see long, deep, and bloody gashes in the flesh located on or near each person's back. Another group consisting almost entirely of Black men meandered along to a destination that only they could have possibly known. This group walked with their heads tilted sharply either to one side or the other. Around their necks were large welts indicating that something had caused significant trauma in that area of their bodies, and was also probably responsible for their slumping heads. Others in this group had features that were completely disfigured, apparently by fire or some other means of inhumane torture. Dumisai's attention was finally caught by a group of White men and women. These people were also in tattered clothes and had emaciated bodies. They looked off into space with a blank stare as if someone or something had left them in betrayal. There was another group that captured Dumisai's attention. It consisted of thousands of Black children with bloated bellies but who were otherwise extremely thin. Still another group consisting of men, women, and children, some with missing hands or feet and others with partial arms and legs which were still bloody, hobbled around. The troubled scenes seemed to go on forever.

Dumisai was in horror at the site in front of him. His mouth, which had been left hanging open from astonishment involuntarily uttered a single word: "No". One simple syllable, as inaudible as it was to Dumisai's own ears, must have sounded more like an explosion to these suffering masses, for they all stopped immediately in their tracks and turned in the direction of the boy. It was as though there was the sudden realization that someone was still whole and physically intact among them. The discovery caused the wretched souls to start a desperate scramble towards Dumisai. The sudden change of events caught Dumisai by surprise and he panicked momentarily as the mass of people attempted to quickly move in his direction. After what seemed like a lifetime, his fear finally released its grip on his muscles, allowing him to move from the spot where he had been standing. He turned to run, hoping to get as far away from the scene as possible, only to discover more of the suffering souls behind him. As far as he could see, there were people all around, and they were starting to close in on all sides. With no place to run to, Dumisai was helpless to do anything besides wait for the inevitable. Attempting to control his panic, he looked closely into the faces of the approaching people. They all had a look of torment about them, but none really appeared to be threatening. As they got closer, Dumisai noticed that they appeared to be gesturing to him for help. They stopped just short of touching him with their arms outstretched but had a look of desperation on their faces.

Dumisai's fear was now replaced by confusion, for what could *he* possibly do to help these poor, desperate souls. They never uttered a sound except for the continuous moaning that must have been an indication of their unrelenting pain. Some of those in the front fell to their knees in an obvious display of desperation, begging the boy for help. Dumisai was moved by the outpouring of emotion directed toward him and wanted to help in any way that he could. He thought about everything that he had been taught since his initiation process began—surely he must have learned something that could help him in this situation, otherwise the old woman would not have sent him into the room. Of all that he had studied nothing seemed to apply to the situation.

Standing just in front of Dumisai, at the edge of the massive crush of victims, was a young woman who had probably been no more than sixteen at the time of her unfortunate demise. She was obviously in torment as she clutched her bloodied mid-section with one hand. Still on her knees, she reached out, lunging for the bag which was slung over Dumisai's shoulder. The sudden action caused the boy to step back instinctively while securing the bag with his hand. After momentarily directing his attention to the object of the woman's desire, he looked closer at her, attempting to find an answer to the lingering question of why she had wanted his bag. Her eyes were completely lifeless even as she stared into his. In her tortured existence, she appeared completely lost, gravitating toward anything or anyone that represented a change from what had become her normal state of existence. Her lost, empty eyes triggered a memory in Dumisai. He recalled what Manzalele had told him: "Sometimes our energies get out of balance and must be brought back into harmony with the whole, lest we risk spending an eternity lost to our true purpose for existence. And that is to realize our divinity and reunite with the source of our being."

Dumisai reached into the bag slung over his shoulder and retrieved an herbal mixture that was kept in a small container. He poured out a few drops of the concoction in each of the four directions while kneeling to the earth to offer a prayer for the uncounted thousands that were suffering. He prayed for peace in the lives of those tormented souls and then grabbed the small canister of water and poured a libation for all the people that had come before him, praising them for their strength, courage, sacrifice and contributions. He asked the Creator to guide their souls so that they could escape their suffering and find peace.

When he finished, Dumisai watched as the masses of people began to turn and walk away, apparently satisfied. Their moaning and wailing stopped and slowly, one by one, they began floating away, blending into the clouds. Dumisai stayed and watched until the last soul had vanished into the atmosphere before turning to inspect his surroundings. He was surprised to find that he was standing across from the door entrance to the room that he had entered at Manzalele's hut. Looking around, he could not find any evidence of the man cowering in the corner, but the remains of the broken pots that had been hurled across the room towards him were still there. He inspected the broken glass just as a reality check and then headed out of the room where he saw Manzalele occupying herself by preparing some food. It was as if she was oblivious to all that he had just experienced.

"So," she said without looking up from her work, "you are done?"

"Yes," Dumisai replied.

"How was the experience?"

"It was… good," Dumisai articulated, searching for the correct word. "I was scared at first, but then I saw that I was not in any real danger."

"Dumisai, did you learn anything, boy?" Manzalele asked impatiently, as she attempted to pull a meaningful response from the boy.

"Yes, I saw the suffering that men inflict on other men. I don't understand how human beings can treat each other that way?"

"Perhaps, it is because they *are* human, eh?"

"What do you mean?"

"Not long ago you agreed that we are made in the image and likeness of the Creator, isn't that true?"

"Yes."

"Well, if that is true, then why must we accept the frailty of a human being as the standard of what is good and right when we are divine beings by nature?"

"Yes, of course… that does make sense," Dumisai acknowledged. "For some reason, I had never thought about it in that way."

"So long as you understand now," Manzalele advised, "that is the important thing. Was there anything else of interest that you experienced?"

"There is one thing—it reminded me of a dream that I keep having."

"A dream…? Hmmm… tell me about it."

"In the dream I am being chased by someone or something. It has no face, yet it's terrifying. It killed my family—not my real family but the people who are supposed to be my family in the dream. They do not look anything like my real family, but I know that is who they are. The creature is after me as well, but so far, I've always awakened just before anything could happen to me. I know that it is only a dream but it seems so real. Oh—I almost forgot…" Dumisai lifted his shirt, "I woke up recently with this scar on my chest."

"Dumisai, why haven't you mentioned this before now?"

"I don't know… I guess I didn't think it was important enough."

Manzalele quickly retrieved her diviner's bag and cast the cowrie shells on the top of the table desk. She studied the arrangement briefly in silence. After she was done, she breathed a deep sigh.

"Dumisai, the dreams you have been having don't have anything to do with restless souls seeking light. Your dreams point to something evil. They are trace memories from a past life of yours. The reason you are experiencing these dreams now is because of a manifestation of evil known as the *Wanga*. The *Wanga* is a spirit that feeds off of hatred and fear. It is attempting to use your dream experiences as a way to attack you psychically. Ultimately, it would like nothing better than to destroy you before you are able to come into manhood and challenge its reign in the world."

"Why is it after me?"

"Dumisai, you still do not know who you are, do you? The light in you shines bright, and that attracts the attention of otherworldly beings. Some of these spirits are watching you, waiting for the opportunity to attack."

"What can I do to guard against these attacks?"

"First and foremost, you must learn to control your emotions. That is the *Wanga's* point of entry into the physical world. It will try to use the fear generated in your dreams as a means to come into the world. Or it will attempt to gain control over a body that can be used as a vessel for evil. Emotions are the fuel that power it. Without a suitable host providing the emotions to fuel it, it is powerless."

"But it is only a dream, right... it's not actually real, is it?"

"Yes, it is a dream, but the dream has been hijacked by something evil. I only hope that it has not already crossed over into this world."

"But what if it has?"

"Then I trust you are ready to apply all that you have learned."

Dumisai gave the old woman a look that was full of concern.

"Worrying accomplishes nothing. You must use the good in you to defeat evil."

"But what if I fail?"

"It is spirit, Dumisai, like everything else. When it comes to dealing with the spirit world you should know by now what resources are at your disposal."

"Yes... I do."

"Good, just trust what you have learned and you will be fine. And remember, always follow proper protocol when dealing with the spirit realm."

"Yes ma'am. I'm sorry if I disappointed you."

"You have nothing to apologize for, boy. You just need to know who you are, is all."

"Yes ma'am."

"Dumisai," the woman said, changing the focus of the conversation, "I know you have been given a lot to digest, but my work with you is not yet done. There is one final lesson that you must learn which quite possibly might be the most important lesson you will learn in this lifetime.

But that is something that will have to wait until tomorrow; we've had a long day already."

Dumisai was intrigued but relieved. Not only was he tired and emotionally drained, he was starting to get hungry. He had not eaten anything except for his breakfast ration. Manzalele already knew what the boy was thinking and offered him a large plate of grapes as well as a couple oranges to appease his appetite.

6: Tree of Secrets

Dumisai awoke to the sound of Manzalele working in her kitchen. She always got up early, just before sunrise, to complete her morning rituals and begin her day. Under ordinary circumstances, she would have awakened Dumisai so that he could learn from observing her, but today she had allowed him to continue sleeping in anticipation of the long day ahead. Realizing that the old woman was already up and about, Dumisai quickly climbed out of bed and headed toward the kitchen where he heard the morning noises coming from. Based on what she had told him the previous day, he was anxious to get started and wondered what new adventure lay in wait for him. Upon entering the kitchen, Dumisai noticed that his plate had already been prepared. As he had come to expect over the last few days, grapes and oranges were to be his meal. Dumisai ate the food that Manzalele had prepared and then downed a large glass of water.

Rising from the table, Dumisai was expecting the old woman to provide some direction on what he should do next. Instead, she continued working in the kitchen, allowing Dumisai ample time to digest his meal. After finishing her morning work tasks, Manzalele exited the dwelling while motioning for Dumisai to follow. She retrieved a bag about the size of a purse from next to the hut before heading into the nearby woods. Dumisai followed obediently. Seeing Manzalele venture into the forest rekindled the intrigue that had captured his imagination concerning the possibilities that the day held in store for him. Perhaps she had saved the best for last, he thought to himself. He allowed his imagination to run free, conjuring up images of the woman tutoring him as he practiced moving objects around, or instructing him on how to transfer his spirit into different animals. As his anticipation continued to grow, Dumisai could hardly maintain his patience. Finally, the old woman came to a clearing which was located in close proximity to the river. In the middle of the clearing stood a large tree that reached well into the air. The area looked familiar but appeared to have been recently cleared of much of the surrounding underbrush. Upon first glance, the large tree looked as though it might have belonged to the oak family yet something about it was different. Its leaves appeared to change right in front of Dumisai as he looked on, making it difficult to identify the tree's species. The lowest branches were well out of reach, hindering the boy's attempts to get a closer view.

"Sit down here," Manzalele instructed, directing Dumisai to a spot at the edge of the clearing. "This space must be purified."

She went to the edge of the river to wash her hands in the water. After she finished, she returned to the clearing and began performing a ritual of purification around the tree. She retrieved a powdery substance from her medicine bag which she poured on the ground at each of the four corners around the clearing, then used a match to light each pile, causing it to smolder with a aromatic plume of smoke. As she walked slowly back and forth, first sprinkling some water also taken from her bag, then retracing her steps to sprinkle ashes until she was satisfied with the distribution of the substance. While doing the various tasks, she never ceased mumbling words in a language that Dumisai could not understand. He watched intently, trying to make sense of her actions by comparing it to what he had learned from the different lessons that she had given him. Finally, the old woman made her way to the center of the clearing where she squatted near the base of the tree. Dumisai was now able to hear her clearly vocalize some words that sounded like *"Hot"* three times while snapping her fingers vigorously. Finally, after the ritual was complete, Manzalele motioned to Dumisai to come close as she waited by the tree.

"Here Dumisai…," she said pointing to the tree, "this is where you will find the answers to life's greatest mysteries."

"In a tree…?" Dumisai asked incredulously.

"Haven't you learned yet that you can't always judge a thing by its outward appearance, boy?" she snapped back, allowing a hint of frustration to creep into her voice.

"Yes, I'm sorry. I should know better by now," the boy offered apologetically.

The tree had a huge trunk and evidently had been there for a long period of time. Its age had not affected its ability to grow lush, green foliage however, for it appeared to be thriving and full of life.

"This tree is special, Dumisai. Ordinarily, a tree of this size would have to be well over a hundred years old, but this tree has been here for no more than ten years. I know because I planted it myself."

"What kind of tree is it?" Dumisai asked.

"It wasn't planted with seeds lad, but with magic. This is a *Tree of Mysteries*. It is unlike any other tree that you will ever encounter."

"What do you mean—*magic*?" Dumisai questioned, his curiosity piqued.

"I'm not talking about some illusionary trick, Dumisai. The magic I'm speaking about requires using spiritual means to manipulate activity on the physical plane. But, in order for one to become a magician, he must properly prepare his spirit, eh?"

"Yes... I believe I understand."

"Believe? No, Dumisai—belief is no good. You must know."

"Yes, ma'am. So... is that why you brought me here... to learn magic?"

"I brought you here to prepare you for your life's work, Dumisai. I have been performing rituals for many years in anticipation of your coming. Now, the time has finally arrived."

Manzalele maneuvered her bent body directly adjacent to the opening in the trunk of the tree.

"Do you see this large hole here at the bottom of this tree?" Manzalele queried, redirecting the boy's focus to the trunk of the tree.

"Yes, it looks like some animal has made a home out of it," the boy answered.

"No boy, that is how it grew. If you look inside of the hole, you will see it is hollow about a third of the distance up."

Dumisai moved in close by the tree so that he could look inside but his face was met with a thick, fog-like swirl at the opening. Hesitating momentarily, the memory of the two squirrels playing and losing their acorns in the tree hollow came back to him, causing him to realize where he had seen the tree before. His intrigue increasing, Dumisai inserted his head fully into the tree and peered upward to verify what the woman had told him, yet the darkness inside of the opening was impenetrable.

"You must enter the tree, Dumisai. Climb up until you reach the top of the hollowed out portion. Then you must wait quietly and reflect on all that you have learned. I will let you know when you are to return."

Dumisai was convinced that there was something special about the tree, but the thought of entering the thick, black swirl inside of it made him hesitant. Still, he did not want to give the impression that he was being disobedient, so he got down onto his hands and knees and prepared to enter the hole at the base of the tree. Manzalele did not hesitate once she gave her instructions. She reached into her bag and retrieved what looked like a smoking pipe. Before Dumisai entered the tree opening, he watched as she poured one of her special packs of powder into the cup portion of the pipe and lit it with a match before sitting down on the ground to enjoy what looked like a good smoke.

Satisfied that the old woman was not going to do anything other than wait for him to follow her instructions and complete his task, Dumisai crawled into the hole at the bottom of the tree with the smell of lavender wafting through the air from the pipe and smoldering piles of dust still lingering in his nostrils. Once inside, he waited for a moment to give his eyes an opportunity to adjust to the darkness before standing slowly in order to keep from bumping his head. Convinced that his eyes had adjusted as much as possible inside the blackness of the tree trunk, he glanced down at the ground, expecting it to be slightly illuminated from the light entering through the opening. To his surprise, the darkness had concealed even his feet. It was as though the opening at the base of the tree had been closed behind him. Within the blackness of the tree, Dumisai's courage began to give way to fear. He could not help but notice the stealthy silence which surrounded him, amplifying the sound of his own heartbeat. The sound of his pounding heart only served to heighten his anxiety, causing him to feel trapped in the darkness. As his fear slowly approached the edge of panic, Dumisai considered abandoning the effort altogether. Suddenly, he heard a soft calming voice inside of the tree coming from somewhere above his head.

"DO NOT BE AFRAID, DUMISAI," persuaded the gentle voice, *"YOU ARE NEVER ALONE."*

The familiarity of the voice was reassuring and helped to allay his fear as he briefly contemplated who it could possibly be. Looking up in search of its source, Dumisai saw a faint glow several feet above his head. The combination of seeing the light and hearing the voice gave him the courage that he needed. He began feeling around the inside of the tree trunk searching for a means to climb up within the hollow. His eyes still could not penetrate the darkness that immediately surrounded him so he continued feeling around hoping to find something to grasp onto. Before long he found a series of notched-out, step-like supports that he was able to grab onto. Oddly enough, finding the step-supports in the tree did not surprise him. For some reason he half expected them to be there. He simply thought that someone must have used the tree for an exercise similar to this one before, and had taken the time to make the entire process a little more convenient.

Dumisai climbed the tree steps toward the light hovering above his head until he realized that he was not getting any closer to its source. Seeing no other alternative, he continued climbing until he became convinced that he should be well past the height of the hollowed out section of the tree. Still the steps continued upward and Dumisai followed, remembering the old woman's instructions. After climbing several feet more, he was sure that he should be nearing the top of the tree by now. He looked above for the light again but was surprised to see that it had disappeared. Looking around he spotted it again, this time out in front of him but still far off in the distance. That doesn't make sense, he thought. How could the light be so far away and still be located inside of the tree trunk? Dumisai reached out to check for the wall of the tree trunk but discovered that it was no longer there. Instead, he was able to feel a flat surface directly in front of him; it seemed to be a ledge of some sort which he was able to pull himself up onto. The darkness was unyielding. His eyes were still attempting to adjust to the lack of lighting, so he proceeded with caution on top of the surface. As he crawled toward the light he noticed that it was beginning to increase in size and intensity as he got closer to it, yet it still was not of a sufficient amount to illuminate the surrounding area. Soon he was standing just before the glowing orb which was now slightly taller than himself. As he stood next to the light, he felt compelled to enter as if he was being pulled into the orb. Unable to resist its beckoning, Dumisai slowly stepped into the circle of light. Once inside, he could see the landscape of a beautiful countryside beneath the soft blue sky unfolding before him. Its beauty was breathtaking yet serene and peaceful.

Dumisai stood motionless in his tracks, attempting to take in the incredible beauty of the view. Looking around, there was no sign that the huge tree which had served as his gateway to this place had even existed. Nor was there anything to suggest that the scenery had ever been spoiled at all. It was the closest thing to paradise that he could have imagined. He felt at once connected to the landscape. His first instinct was to explore. He walked a short distance before noticing the alluring waters of a wide and peaceful river in front of him. Following the expanse of the waters, he saw a huge waterfall off in the distance. The waterfall seemed so majestic. It was so tall and wide that he desperately wanted to get close enough to experience its beauty firsthand.

As he began moving toward the roaring waters, he found himself suddenly standing knee deep in the river near the base of the falls. It was as if the waters had anticipated his thoughts and instantly transported him there, positioning him securely on some platform submerged beneath the water's surface. The falls thundered down now only a few yards in front of him. Still drawn by the lure of the waterfall, Dumisai couldn't resist the urge to enter into the cascading waters, fully aware that he might be pummeled by their mighty force. As he stepped toward the flowing waters, he was oblivious to the platform beneath him that was supporting his weight. Unable to halt his progress while under the spell of the alluring waters, he entered into the streaming downpour expecting to be pounded into the river by the impact and then be swept away in the churning foam of the stirring waters. Instead, he experienced an exhilarating sensation which coursed through his body. He welcomed the blissful feeling before finally surrendering to the calming relaxation that overcame him. The water was warm and soothing as though its entire reason for being was for the purpose of nurturing life. The gentle caress of the cascading falls was comforting as it washed across his skin. Dumisai felt safe surrounded by its warm embrace and did not want to leave. The experience triggered something deeply rooted in his psyche causing him to recall some of the earliest moments of his childhood. As the thought continued to build in his mind, a vision began to form in front of him. It was a floating mass, indistinguishable in form, just beyond the reach of his hands, yet still within the downpour of the torrent. He watched as the mass began to take on a shape that finally became recognizable as an unborn fetus. After only a few moments the newly formed fetus had become distinguishable as human. Dumisai's initial thought was to reach out to touch the unborn baby yet something was preventing him. He contented himself to watch as the baby continued to grow and develop right before his eyes. The fetus quickly completed its prenatal development until finally it was ready to be born. With a flash of light the baby's fetal position changed and the child was standing upright, suspended in mid-air, still growing but now as a newborn infant. The growth of the child held Dumisai's attention as it transitioned from infant to toddler to pre-school age. As it continued to grow, the speed of the progression began to slow down and Dumisai began to see familiarity in the face of the individual that he had been watching. His suspicions were confirmed when the age progression finally came to a stop. The child whom he had been watching was an exact replica of himself. The newly-formed child did not appear to notice his presence at all. It assumed a meditative posture as it continued to hover suspended in the air. Within moments, seed-like particles materialized around the meditating child and began bombarding it with a continuous stream that disappeared upon contact as if being absorbed into the child's body. Finally, the particle-stream slowed to a trickle and the body of the duplicate child began to emit a soft, white glow. The glow gradually intensified, emitting rays of bright white light until Dumisai was forced to shield his eyes in an attempt to protect them. Then the entire scene was gone as suddenly as it had appeared.

Released from his stupor, Dumisai looked around for the duplicate of himself and the waterfall but saw nothing but complete darkness. He waited for his eyes to finish adjusting following the intense glare that had accompanied the light, but was still unable to see anything. He wondered briefly if he had been permanently blinded until he spotted another light-circle. It was identical to the one he had seen back in the hollowed out tree. He reached out to feel his way around and was surprised to find what felt like more notched-out steps. Assuming that he had no other choice, he climbed the steps to see if they would lead him to the light. As he ascended the steps, Dumisai could feel the urge increasing to enter into the light circle as he approached closer to it. After reaching the edge of the light, he stepped into the sphere without hesitating. Immediately upon entering, he was transported to another place in time. Looking around, he could see that there were thousands of people gazing upon him and cheering loudly. Within moments of arriving he had somehow become the object of everyone's attention. The crowd, which had worked itself into a frenzy, began chanting in unison, "DU-MI-SAI!... DU-MI-SAI!... DU-MI-SAI!... DU-MI-SAI!..."

As the noise level increased to a deafening roar, Dumisai took time to survey his surroundings. He was seated in an oversized chair which was not only too big for him, but was also located upon an elevated stage which separated it from the masses of people by several yards. He also noticed that he was dressed in strange garments which included a red and white tunic trimmed in gold, as well as an odd-shaped red crown that resembled a small, legless chair with a tall back which became narrow toward the top. In one hand he held a jackal-headed scepter, and in the other an object resembling a Christian Cross except it was constructed with an oval loop on top. The smell of frankincense swirled about his nostrils as six men approached from his right flank before stopping to kneel in front of him.

"My lord," one of the men said upon rising to his feet, "we seek your guidance in this hour of need against the dark forces that have once again risen up in rebellion."

Instinctively, Dumisai knew what to do as if he had lived his entire life in preparation for this moment. The words, the gestures, all seemed to come to him intuitively. He felt comfortable in the role, as if all was happening just as it was supposed to. "Prepare my armaments," the boy responded authoritatively while standing to face the cheering crowd. One of the men quickly left in response to his request. As Dumisai approached the edge of the stage, the mere sight of him sent the crowd into a frenzy of cheers. He looked out upon all who had come to see him and raised his right hand confidently acknowledging their appreciation and acceptance of his role as their leader. Before turning to leave, he summoned the remaining men of the six that had originally approached him. "These rebels," Dumisai acknowledged, "where can I find them?"

"They gather just beyond the gateway to the kingdom, my lord, waiting for any opportune moment to attack." As the man spoke, his contemporary returned with a bow, a quiver of arrows, and a stylized dagger which he gave to Dumisai.

"Your chariot awaits, my lord," the helper informed.

Dumisai thanked the men for their service as he exited to the rear of the stage. He turned to give a final glance behind him before leaving, but was surprised to find that the crowd had disappeared. No longer could he hear the bellowing roar of his name, nor did he see any of the people or objects that had been before him only moments ago. He searched all around but could not find any evidence that the previous scene had even occurred except for the strange garments that he still wore. He held the bow in his hands with the dagger tucked neatly into a sheath. The stage that he had stood upon only moments before had been replaced by a sand dune. Behind him, he could see in the distance the historic pyramids of the ancient Egyptian civilization. In place of the cheering crowd standing before him, he now saw only a giant serpent, upon whose neck was sitting what appeared to be a sorcerer wearing a black cloak trimmed in red. Atop the cloak was a hood that shrouded the sorcerer's face in shadow. Dumisai stared curiously at the serpent-beast and its rider. The giant serpent hissed threateningly and then coiled as though preparing to strike, but instead gently lowered its master to the ground. The sorcerer immediately raised his hand skyward, directing the serpent into action. The creature obeyed by rising up on its tail, extending a full eighteen feet high. As it towered over Dumisai, the serpent-beast flicked its forked-tongue menacingly while eyeing the boy like he was some prized prey. Dumisai took a step closer to the giant snake, undaunted by its size or its threatening action. Surprised by the boy's display of courage, the sorcerer responded by raising both hands, commanding the serpent to strike. It obeyed by spreading the skin of its neck in a manner resembling a hooded cobra before making a quick strike. Dumisai calmly anticipated the attack and dived elusively into a forward roll, avoiding the venomous fangs of the creature before coolly arming his bow with an arrow. Recoiling, the serpent quickly lunged again, intent on crushing the boy within its powerful jaws. Immediately, it retracted, emitting a loud, agonizing shriek as it reared its head high into the air, trying desperately to dislodge the black obsidian arrowhead from the roof of its mouth. The giant serpent writhed in agony before it finally collapsed, landing with a loud thud against the ground and then slowly disintegrated into a mass of squirming, worm-like creatures that disappeared into the dust.

"NOOOO!!!" the sorcerer screamed, unable to contain his rage after witnessing the turn of events. "Young, arrogant upstart! You will pay for this!"

The sorcerer raised his scepter skyward as he prepared to mount his next attack. "Come, my children. The time for you to demonstrate your allegiance has arrived!"

As Dumisai looked around, he saw a horde of creatures approaching from over the crest of the hill. They were short in statue, almost resembling dwarfs except each had the head of an animal instead of a person. There were scores of the diminutive creatures that surrounded Dumisai.

"ATTACK, my legion!!!" the sorcerer commanded. "Strike the insolent Rex and let him know who is the rightful ruler of the land! Go now and bring me the heart of the man-child that I may feast on it!"

A wave of the dwarf-creatures attacked Dumisai.

"Do not tarry my rebellious children!" the sorcerer exclaimed, "for your master commands you!"

Before Dumisai could react, the miniature animal-headed men were upon him, piling on top until he was completely covered by a mass of small bodies. The number was too great to overcome, making it useless for Dumisai to resist. Instead, he allowed himself to sink to the earth under the weight of the creatures. The sorcerer laughed with satisfaction as he celebrated the boy's apparent demise. As he gloated arrogantly, a sudden gust of wind blew the hood off of his head, revealing the head of an anteater with large donkey-like ears and fire-red eyes.

Several moments passed as Dumisai lay motionless beneath the heap of miniature bodies. He thought he was losing consciousness as he felt his body becoming weightless. The sensation was strange yet inviting, leaving him feeling as if he was floating. Once he opened his eyes, he could see the mass of bodies beneath him. At that moment he realized that he was hovering above the scene which was still taking place on the ground. The dwarf-sized creatures were still jostling for position on the pile, attempting to finish the job that they had begun. Looking closer, Dumisai managed to spot his own body which was still lying lifeless under the crush of the creatures below him. As he looked around the area, he saw the sorcerer still watching the scramble of activity on the ground with an obvious look of satisfaction adorning his face. Dumisai quickly discovered that just by thinking he was able to propel his floating form around. He willed his astral form over the sorcerer, wielding his dagger with its razor sharp, curved-tip blade. After positioning his astral body directly behind the head of the sorcerer, he swung the double-edged implement with all of the might he could muster, severing the head from the body of the fiend. The sorcerer's head rolled across the desert sand, landing next to the heap of animal-headed creatures and leaving the headless body to stagger around clumsily. Finally, the body of the sorcerer fragmented, dispersing hundreds of black crows which flew off in every direction. With no master to direct them, the dwarf-creatures scattered in confusion, leaving the boy's pummeled body behind. Dumisai looked down at his inert body still lying on the ground and then immediately re-entered his crumpled physical form which lay listless on the sand, only to be instantly swept away.

Dumisai was again transported back to the place where he found himself lost in total darkness. Still unable to see inside of the black hollow, he instinctively felt for his garments to determine if the snake episode had indeed ended. As he suspected, his strange clothing was gone, replaced by his normal attire. He turned his attention upward, expecting to find a circle of light awaiting him. His suspicions proved to be correct, for the glowing orb seemed to be waiting specifically for his ascent. He reached out into the darkness anticipating the steps. Again his suspicions proved to be accurate. Dumisai ascended the steps toward the light. This time, without hesitation of thought, he stepped into the light. He was sure that this was yet another lesson that the old woman had prepared for him.

Entering the light, Dumisai expected to be whisked away again to some strange place, but instead he remained there in the darkness. He looked for the light circle but it was nowhere to be found. Not knowing where to turn, Dumisai remembered the old woman's instructions to wait and reflect on what he had been taught. After a few minutes, he again attempted to peer through the darkness and this time was able to spot a faint white light far off in the distance. The light was very small and barely noticeable as Dumisai stared at it for several seconds, wanting to make sure of its existence before proceeding forward. Finally convinced that he wasn't seeing things, the boy began to feel his way through the darkness toward the light. As he got closer, the light became brighter, illuminating the side of a mountain upon which it was sitting. The mountain appeared to be white also, apparently covered in snow. Dumisai walked until he reached the foot of the elevation and proceeded to climb up. The white substance covering it was not cold to the touch, though it otherwise had the texture of snow. Other than the mountain and the light source sitting atop it, Dumisai found it difficult to see anything beyond the crevices that he used for climbing. When he finally reached the peak and was able to approach the source of its luminance, he came upon an oval object about the size of a bowling ball that appeared to be an egg floating above the ground. The object illuminated the immediate area, surrounding itself with bright white light. Dumisai looked around to see what else he might be able to view using the light emanating from the object, but except for the egg-shaped object itself and its immediate surroundings, he was unable to see anything. He reached out and gently grabbed the object, finding it to be both smooth and lightweight, exactly like an egg. To his surprise he was able to handle it quite easily at first, but then the warm touch of his hands caused the egg to vibrate, sending a surge of energy coursing through his body. He could feel the energy suddenly cascade through his being. Instantly, he was overcome by an urge to live through the experiences of an infinite number of creatures. The subconscious urge quickly gave way to an awareness that allowed him to envisage the oneness of being through a single stream of consciousness. It was a feeling of unity that was much stronger than the simple connection that he had always shared with animals. He was able to perceive every thought, feeling and emotion that drifted through the universe. Dumisai felt as though he was standing in space looking down on the whole earth, yet free to be anyone or anything and anywhere by merely willing it to be so. The feeling was electric. Every possible sensation washed over him, yet he was unmoved. He witnessed thousands of thoughts enter and exit his consciousness as he embraced the liberating sense of freedom that accompanied the experience. There was nothing that could constrain his being. His awareness increased until his consciousness finally merged with the infinite expanse of the universe itself. The cosmic encounter lasted only a few seconds and then his consciousness suddenly rejoined his physical body.

Dumisai needed a moment to recover from the stupefying experience while he attempted to get his bearings. Finally, he realized that he was still standing in the black void which was slightly illuminated by the glowing egg that he still held in his hands. He longed for the feeling of unity again but was forced to redirect his attention back to the glowing orb which had begun to tremble violently as if it was ready to crack open. He watched in anticipation, waiting to see what would hatch from the glowing egg-like object. After several seconds of shaking violently, the object finally cracked open to reveal nothing but an empty blackness. Dumisai stared into the emptiness expecting to find something that he could have possibly overlooked, but the blackness inside of the shell was all that was there. Looking closer, he noticed that the blackness had some motion to it. The movement was slow, but Dumisai was sure that it existed. It reminded him of the swirl that oozed out of the opening of the hollow in the tree. It began to swirl slowly until it crept over the side of the broken shell engulfing its white light in the process. Dumisai was startled momentarily and dropped the broken eggshell to his feet. The black swirl continued unabated, now completely consuming both the light from the shell and even the remaining darkness that surrounded the boy. Soon Dumisai himself was completely engulfed in the swirl. He could feel himself losing his bearings as the swirl continued to move in a circular pattern all around him. He felt as though he was falling, his body starting to tumble out of control. It was impossible to see anything during the freefall, even his hands which were just in front of his face had been replaced by blackness. Except for his thoughts, there was nothing to validate that he even still existed. The black swirl was all there was. Perhaps his body had disintegrated, he thought, and become one with the swirling mass. Yet he was able to remain conscious of his own existence which was now inseparable from the swirl itself. Unable to resist the force of swirling energy, he finally submitted to the freefall, riding out the black swirl and then finally becoming part of it. A faint sound just barely audible penetrated the blackness and made its way into his consciousness. As he drifted effortlessly with the movement of the swirl, the sound increased in intensity, gradually growing louder and louder until the once faint buzz became a loud, consistent hum. The humming noise continued to resonate, vibrating as if it had been initiated in an echo chamber and droning monotonously until it became inseparable from the blackness. As it permeated the whole of the black swirl, it caused the smooth circular motion to become disturbed until the intensity of the constant ringing sensation caused by the vibration became too much for Dumisai to bear, causing him to lose consciousness.

Finally, he awoke. Dumisai had no means of gauging how long he had been unconscious. Upon opening his eyes, he realized that he was able to see again. He carefully checked his hands, legs and feet as if he was verifying that all his parts were still there. As he checked his surroundings, he noticed that he was lying on the ground with his feet still inside the opening of the hollowed out tree while the rest of his body was jutting just out of the tree cavity. He must be back then, he thought, as his eyes searched the area for more familiar signs to confirm his suspicion. As he slowly climbed to his feet, he saw Manzalele sitting by the tree, swaying back and forth as though she had the aid of an unseen rocking chair. Watching the old woman rocking to and fro with her eyes closed, he thought that she might be in throes of some nightmare. As he slowly approached her, he was able to detect a strange sound emanating from her lips. He listened carefully to her vocalization as he attempted to identify the sound he was hearing. The realization came that the strange noise escaping her lips was the same sound that he had heard in the tree. There was no mistaking what he was hearing. It had been her all along, he thought, calling for him to return. Dumisai dared not disturb the woman as he continued watching her. Finally, as if she had detected his presence, Manzalele sat upright and became still, and then suddenly opened her eyes which were rolled back in her head. The sight combined with the sudden action caused Dumisai to jump back, momentarily startled.

"So, it is done," Manzalele declared, ignoring the boy's reaction and adjusting her eyes so that she could see. "My work with you is now complete."

"So… what happens now?" Dumisai inquired, attempting to regain his composure.

Manzalele slowly climbed to her feet, relying on her staff to support her weight as she maneuvered her bent-over body into the semblance of an upright stance.

"First, you must complete your initiation, eh?" she reminded. Her eyes seemed to look past Dumisai to some other object which had caught her attention.

Dumisai recognized that her attention had temporarily focused elsewhere even though she was still speaking to him. He turned slowly, following the direction of her stare. His eyes met those of the *Chikunza* who was standing directly behind him. Dumisai knew now that his apprenticeship under the tutelage of the old woman was over. He gave a final glance back at Manzalele as if awaiting some final confirmation from her. She offered a simple nod which was the signal he needed to confirm that he was to accompany the ancestor spirit back to its destination.

The *Chikunza* guided Dumisai back to the initiation camp. When they arrived at the enclosure, Sasombo was waiting by the gate to usher him into the camp. The attendants were anticipating Dumisai's return and had already prepared lessons in order to continue from where they had left off so that the initiation process could be completed.

The days seemed to go by swiftly now that the initiation was nearing completion. Dumisai was thrilled when the elders finally painted his body with the customary geometric symbols. He could feel the excitement building in the camp as the men began to celebrate with millet beer. Malekazi instructed Dumisai to dress in a grass-kilt skirt that had been specially prepared for him and provided the boy with a cone-shaped hat and a walking staff. The men attending the campsite gathered all of their belongings before finally beginning the march with Dumisai back in the direction of the village. A few attendants remained behind and set fire to the campsite, erasing any remaining sign of the secret knowledge which had been shared there. Dumisai could hear the men celebrating while they stayed behind tending to the fire. He didn't bother looking back because the camp symbolized his childhood and he was now focused on the next stage of life.

Once he made his triumphant return to the village accompanied by the escorts, Dumisai was greeted by a throng of revelers happy to see that he had made it back. Their once reticent child had been reborn into manhood. Malaika beamed when she saw her son. He had been gone for too long in her opinion, but she knew that his journey signaled the end of his childhood and would require a different type of interaction from her going forward. The entire village had gathered to join in the celebration welcoming Dumisai home. His successful completion of the *Mukanda* initiation process represented a milestone occurrence in the village. The fact that they had successfully incorporated an important aspect of their cultural heritage into their new world village settlement was a legitimate reason to celebrate. Dumisai was led to a spot prepared especially for him and presented with a feast to celebrate his return. He ate well. He knew the celebration would follow soon and that he would be called upon to demonstrate some of the dances he had learned. He found a spot to rest as he observed the pride exhibited by the villagers for the life they had created for themselves.

7: Council of Elders

Dumisai's body refused to cooperate as he attempted to leave the comfort of his bed. The physical and psychological strain resulting from the *Mukanda* initiation process had left him tired and emotionally drained. Even with the physical exhaustion, he still had been unable to get a good, restful night's sleep. After lying awake for several more minutes, he managed to finally crawl out of bed and stumble to his wash-bucket. So much had happened to him that he had not yet had an opportunity to process it all. He needed to sort through his thoughts before facing the elders in the special council meeting that had been called on his behalf. After washing his face, Dumisai stepped outside to avoid waking his parents who were still asleep. The sun was just beginning to ascend the eastern horizon and the brisk autumn air brought an unexpected boost of energy which helped to recharge his spirit. He took in a deep breath, filling his lungs with the fresh, clean air of the outdoors and then exhaled slowly in an attempt to clear his mind of all the thoughts which were starting to converge inside of his head. He used the moment of clarity to begin ordering his thoughts so that he could make sense of the different events which had led him to his fate. Dumisai needed to prepare himself mentally for the council meeting in order to present his best possible face to the elders. He didn't know why they wanted to speak to him but was sure that his manhood training had been successfully completed. The initiation camp had been burned according to tradition and he had been marched back into the village as a fully initiated man. At least, that was what he thought constituted the completion of his rite of passage into manhood. Yet, for some reason unknown to him, the Council of Elders still wanted an audience with him.

Dumisai passed the time waiting for the start of the council meeting by returning to the river. It was the one place where he could always go when he wanted to forget about any thoughts that were crowding his mind. Of all the things that he could choose to do to get away from the challenges of life, he still found sitting by the water to be the most peaceful and relaxing. He could always count on its calming presence to transport his mind to some serene and distant location away from the pressing issues of the moment. Once he reached the shore, Dumisai sat down to observe the water as it flowed effortlessly downstream, washing over and around the river rocks on its journey toward its final destination. He spotted a medium-sized rock along the shore which he grabbed and tossed high into the air, allowing it to come down into the river with a loud *splunk*. He watched as the splash from the stone and the resulting ripples travelled outward before finally disappearing into the watery expanse. Observing the simple elegance of the interplay between the water and the surrounding natural formations, Dumisai allowed his thoughts to drift unimpeded, resisting every urge to focus on any one in particular. Finally, he allowed the water to remind him of the lessons shared with him by his grandmother. He was amazed at how something which was so completely yielding when at peace and conformed to the shape of any vessel imposed upon it, could represent such a powerful force that was worthy of the respect of even the earth's mightiest creatures. Even in its peaceful state it had the potential to allow one's aggression to cause their own demise without ever changing its form or character. Yet, it could also be completely overbearing, smashing anything in its path if stirred up by either natural or manmade forces. Dumisai marveled at the respect that it was able to command. Something seemingly so simple yet representing so much more that was complex in the universe. This force of power—whether at peace or manifesting its potential to destroy—was a lot like man because it represented both the meek and the powerful all at once. Of everything in nature that he had observed, Dumisai enjoyed water most of all. It not only provided a peaceful escape, but also offered a great lesson on life.

The elders had already gathered at the meeting place when Dumisai arrived during the mid-afternoon hours. He wondered how long they had been there and whether he had broken protocol by arriving after the members of the council. As he approached the elders who were seated in a semi-circle formation, his eyes met those of Ol' Manzalele. The stern stare of the woman caused a chill to shoot through his body, momentarily freezing him in his tracks. Dumisai was surprised by his reaction since he thought that he was used to the old woman by now. As he fought back the nervous energy that was trying to swell up in his stomach, he proceeded to the mouth of the circle of elders. Baba Kenje rose to his feet with his hands outstretched to welcome the boy who had stopped just outside of the semi-circle. Kenje's smile was warm and communicated that all was fine. Dumisai immediately kneeled on one knee and bowed his head as a sign of respect to the elders and the council, asking for permission to join the gathering.

"You may enter, Dumisai," Baba Kenje stated, his voice reassuring as always.

Dumisai stepped into the semi-circle and quickly found a spot on the ground where he could sit. As his eyes panned across the group of elders, he could see the wisdom of their many years etched into the wrinkles lining their faces. He had always taken his youth for granted, not stopping to consider that he himself would one day get old. Gazing upon their distinguished features, he wondered how many stories they might tell if they had the notion. They all seemed so serious, yet grandfatherly and approachable. Finally, since he had called the meeting, Baba Kenje took the liberty to address the subject of the council.

"Dumisai, the council is very interested in hearing what you have learned over the course of the last few months. Now, we understand that much of what you've learned was intended for you alone and not meant to be repeated. We are not asking that you share that, however, we do need to know if our process of initiation has satisfied the purpose for which it was intended. You will be asked several questions and your answers will tell us all that we need to know."

"Dumisai," voiced a heavy-set woman who was sitting amongst the elders and apparently uninterested in waiting to get started. "You claim to be a man?"

"Yes ma'am, I am."

"What is your responsibility as such?"

"My responsibility is first to ensure the well-being of my community, then that of my family, and then myself."

"You would place the well-being of the community before your self?" the woman asked, digging deeper.

"Yes—without the community, I am nothing," Dumisai responded.

"Uh huh," the woman replied with a nod, satisfied with the answer that Dumisai had provided.

"Dumisai," spoke an old man with mostly grayed dreadlocks, "explain for the council the authority in charge of this village."

"There is no authority over the God who created the universe," Dumisai began. "Everything that we do is by His permission."

"So, we only do what God allows us?"

"No, we have free will, therefore we are free to make our own choices in life. But if our choices are not based on God's Will then we will have to suffer the consequences that we bring on ourselves."

"How can you know if the choices that you make are indeed God's Will?" the old man pressed.

"We know because God based the world on law when it was created. As long as we obey God's laws, we are doing God's Will."

"And how can one know what is God's laws?"

"We know based on our experience with nature. God's laws are the same as the laws of nature."

"And how can we know that that is true?"

"Our ancestors made observations and verified them over time, and have passed down their knowledge of these laws to us."

"Very good, Dumisai," the dreadlocked man admitted. "I am quite impressed."

"Dumisai," injected another elder, "do you know what your purpose is in life?"

"Yes sir."

"Share with the council what it is that you have come to know."

"I know that God needs me in order to come into the world."

"Can you explain further what you mean?"

"Yes. I must allow God to work through me in order to place the world back on its divine path."

"And how can you be so sure that this is your purpose in life?"

"God spoke to me through the ancestors to remind me of why I came to earth, then, the elder Manzalele confirmed the ancestors' message using the oracle."

"Very well, Dumisai," the elder acknowledged. "You have answered well. That is all."

"Yes, Dumisai," rejoined Baba Kenje, "your answers speak well of your manhood training, and Manzalele has also done a fine job. We are pleased with your progress. Now it is time for you to take your rightful place among us as a man. Come forward."

Dumisai took a step toward Baba Kenje who stood to greet the newly initiated young man. Baba Kenje held in his hands an elaborately carved staff which he placed in Dumisai's outstretched hands.

"Dumisai, I hereby confer to you the title of manhood as sanctioned by the Council of Elders."

Baba Kenje paused briefly as he placed both of his wiry hands across Dumisai's shoulders.

"Listen Dumisai, you have made us proud. Even before your formal initiation, you demonstrated wisdom beyond your years. You are indeed worthy of the title of manhood. Now the time has come for you to leave us. Not as a child seeking to find his way, but as a man—a man who has been initiated into the mysteries of the universe. It is time for you to put into practice all that you have learned."

Dumisai listened stoically as he observed the members of the council looking on approvingly. Seeing the resolute expressions adorning the face of his elders, he could easily imagine God working through them to affect the world.

Baba Kenje paused, allowing Dumisai an opportunity to speak, but the boy's response was only a nod to acknowledge his understanding of the old man's words.

"We will miss you, Dumisai," Kenje continued, "but know that yours is a work ordained by God. By way of the *Gift*, you are able to do things that the average person will only dream about. Use all that you have learned. Allow the ancestors to be your guide, and they will not abandon you. And most important, Dumisai, ask God to lead you when you are faced with difficult choices. The answers may be revealed through various means but they will always be forthcoming. Now that you know what to look for, you are ready to meet your destiny."

If Dumisai was unsure, he did not let on what kind of thoughts might be going through his head. He knew that part of becoming a man meant embracing his destiny and he intended to show that he was capable of doing so.

"I am ready, Baba," Dumisai proclaimed, his voice brimming with confidence. "I am ready to take on my responsibilities as a man, and I will make you and the ancestors proud!"

"We know you will, Dumisai," Baba Kenje assured, "we know you will."

Baba Kenje turned to face the rest of the council before adjourning the meeting. "Alright good people, I think we should be able to wrap this little meeting up now," he proclaimed loudly with a grin. "We don't want to be accused of being too serious around here, do we?"

Dumisai slowly surveyed the faces of each elder. Their expressions remained fixed despite Kenje's attempt at injecting some levity into the occasion. Dumisai knew by their silence that nothing had been left unstated. He could see the approval of every elder on the council and it was obvious that they had arrived at a consensus agreement concerning his future plans. Dumisai was pleased that they were comfortable enough to place their confidence in him and certainly did not want to let them down. He kneeled, coming to rest on one knee before thanking the council for their insight and direction. He then slowly backed out of the semi-circle formation, careful not to allow his back to turn toward the elders until he was at a respectful distance.

Dumisai stopped and waited a moment to see if his parents who had been allowed to attend, were going to follow. Malaika and Bento received the council's permission to be dismissed before making their way over to their son at a normal pace, not wanting to display any sense of urgency. They understood the duty that he had been called upon to carry out in the world and if they were sad that he would soon be leaving them, they did not let it show. Instead, they outwardly expressed their pride at the fact that someone of such importance had come through their bloodline. As they approached Dumisai, he was also careful not to display any outward emotion. He did not want to give his mother cause to worry, nor did he want to give the impression that he was seeking consolation from her as a child. As the council adjourned, he gave his mother a look to reassure her that all would be fine. She smiled back while allowing Bento to place his arm around her shoulders. The three made their way back to their hut for an evening meal. Dumisai would be leaving the next day and his mother wanted to make sure he left home well-nourished.

8: Into The Wilderness

Dumisai rummaged through both knapsacks that his parents had packed for him in preparation for his journey out into the world. While verifying the contents of the bags, he thought of his last meal with them. Everything had seemed so solemn as if everyone had purposely avoided discussing the fact that he would soon be leaving. In fact, the only conversation at all had centered around the food until his mother finally burst into tears, no longer able to maintain her composure. Dumisai comforted her with a hug as she kissed him on his forehead. Malaika then whispered to her son that she loved him and reminded him to be sure to take care of himself while away. His father had not been so dramatic; he simply placed both hands on Dumisai's shoulders, and then looked into his eyes as he told him sternly to remember all the things that he had been taught. Bento then reached into his pocket and retrieved a necklace which he handed to Dumisai. The pendant of the necklace was a smooth, flat stone of black onyx. It was about the size of an Indian arrowhead, and was flanked on each side by six black beads stacked atop each other. The strap which held the stone was thin but strong, being constructed from animal skin into a sturdy leather band.

"This is something that I had been saving to give to you when the time was right, Dumisai. This talisman has been in our family for generations, passed down from father to eldest son. Back home in Angola, when your great, great grandfather was initiated into manhood, this is one of the things that he returned with. Since you are my first born son, it is only fitting that you have this now as you leave us to go and find your own way."

Dumisai bowed to receive the necklace from his father who placed it over his head. "Thank you, Father," Dumisai expressed appreciatively. He then gave both his parents a final hug before retiring to bed for the evening.

While recalling his memories of the previous evening, Dumisai thought fondly about his parents and how much he would miss them. The thought of not having his family nor the village community around while away on his journey would ordinarily make him uncomfortable, but the excitement he felt overshadowed any anxiety that tried to surface. He was eager to begin the adventure and had to make an effort to keep his enthusiasm in check.

Putting his thoughts aside, Dumisai collected all of the items that he believed would be useful on his journey and stuffed them into one of the two bags packed by his mother. She had prepared many items for him to take and had neatly wrapped them into small individual bundles for convenience. In addition to what his mother had prepared for him, Dumisai anticipated finding fruits and berries along the way to help supplement his meals. The town that he would be heading towards was only a few days walk away. Once he got there he hoped to find work by helping some of the businesses with their cleanup responsibilities if necessary. Of course, it all would depend on how long he would have to be there. He had already decided that he would stay however long it was necessary to accomplish his objective.

Dumisai was ready to go before noon. As he prepared to leave the village, the sense of adventure which always accompanied his walks was beginning to build. He had always enjoyed his treks through the woods but this time the feeling that welled up inside him was one of total excitement because of the special purpose that was the reason for the trip. The town that he had set his sights on was called Milling. He could sometimes see some of the town's lights in the distance at night when he went up to Lookout Point on the outskirts of the village. He had already decided that this would be a good place to begin his journey. Slinging his bags over his shoulder, Dumisai looked around the hut to make sure that he had not forgotten any critical item before setting out for the town. He had wanted to tell his parents goodbye, but they were nowhere to be found. He left them a quick note explaining that the time had come for him to leave and that he would hopefully return within a few weeks. Once he got out of the door, only then did he notice the crowd of people that had gathered in the village circle. The group had been waiting for him and upon seeing him exit the hut, opened up to form a human corridor for him to pass through on his way out. At the front of the walkway were his parents, one on each side. As Dumisai walked by, each individual offered words of encouragement which he graciously received. Eventually, he arrived at the end of the line of people that had formed, to where most of the council elders were waiting. Each of the elders maintained a look of seriousness, as though their sole purpose for being there was to remind Dumisai of the importance of his undertaking. Baba Kenje and Manzalele were the last two that he would have to pass. As he walked by, Baba Kenje reached out and placed a hand on the boy's shoulder, causing Dumisai to pause for a moment. Baba Kenje looked into the boy's eyes and then nodded approvingly before allowing him to continue. Dumisai then looked to the old woman for some sign of reassurance, but her expression remained fixed and aloof. He noticed a faraway stare in her pinkish eyes that suggested a preoccupation with some other thought. Unable to gain the attention of the woman, Dumisai continued on. He was glad that the people had taken some time out of their day to see him off. He was especially pleased that his mother and father had taken the time to say goodbye. As he walked away from the village he felt assured that everything was going to be okay.

Dumisai had walked the trail to Lookout Point many times. He had not been in any hurry prior to leaving the village, but now that he was actually on his way to Milling, the excitement he felt motivated him to move quickly so that he might get to his destination as soon a possible. He could hardly wait to see this new place with its many lights and different people. He had been to one of the smaller surrounding towns before with his mother to do some grocery shopping but Milling had always seemed so much bigger. It was the closest thing to a real city around those parts. Until now, Dumisai had never had an interest in going to the city, but as he allowed his curiosity to lead him, the idea of seeing and experiencing new things made it difficult for him to contain his enthusiasm.

As he plodded along the trail to the edge of the forest, Dumisai could see the rock formation atop Lookout Point through the branches of the trees. He knew he would be able to see his destination from the top of the hillside and would let that mark the official start of his journey away from the village. As he approached the clearing at the edge of the forest and eyed the base of the hill, a sudden uncomfortable feeling came over him. He felt as if he was being watched. Dumisai cautiously looked around, attempting to pinpoint the source of the sudden uneasiness that he was experiencing. He continued along his path toward the hill, carefully searching the shadows cast by the various rocks and trees for anything that seemed out of place. Not finding anything upon which to base his suspicions, he continued his march up the hill. The nearer to the top that he climbed, the stronger the feeling became. A presence seemed to pervade the atmosphere as if the air itself was thick with some insidious energy. Despite the troublesome feeling, Dumisai continued pressing forward. Without any real justification for turning back, he was determined to continue on his journey in order to complete his mission.

After finally reaching the top of the hill, Dumisai saw what he suspected had caused him to feel watched. The eyes of a gray wolf were trained directly on his every move. The animal had a menacing look about it, crouching close to the ground as it carefully stalked Dumisai, circling slowly as if readying for an attack. He wanted to try communicating with the animal but something seemed to be interfering with his ability to gain the animal's cooperation. He knew he had to keep trying even though he was sure that something wasn't right about the animal.

"You... wolf, why are you stalking me?"

There was no answer. In fact, the malevolent energy seemed to be even stronger than before, exciting the strange acting wolf to action as it came closer in preparation to attack.

"Wolf!?! What's wrong with you?! Why don't you answer?!"

Still no answer. The animal's behavior was beginning to make Dumisai very uneasy. As he looked closer at the wolf's snarling face, Dumisai finally noticed the saliva that was foaming around the corners of the animal's mouth. He knew that was a signal that the wolf might be sick and very dangerous. He slowly began backing away from the top of the hill. For each step backwards that he took, the animal menacingly stalked forward, growling and baring its teeth. Dumisai knew he could not outrun the animal but felt he had no choice. He turned quickly, attempting to sprint back down the hill just as the wolf attacked. Saliva spewed from the mouth of the wolf as it leaped, sensing that it was ready to make the young man its prey. Dumisai already knew that his attempt to flee was futile but instinctively attempted to dive out of the crazed animal's path when he heard a thud and a simultaneous yelp directly above his body. He rolled over quickly, returning to a half upright stance on one knee, ready to dash away again if necessary. A ferocious fight was occurring right in front of him between the rabid wolf and another animal. Dumisai quickly recognized that the animal which had come to his apparent rescue was itself a wolf. A large, white wolf.

The fight was fierce with the two animals rolling violently across the ground, each attempting to gain an advantage with its speed and strength in order to get a good snap at the other's jugular. Finally, a loud yelp pierced the air and then the fight was over. Dumisai watched as the white wolf limped away from its dead adversary. Its whimper suggesting that it too had been hurt during the fight as it sought out a comfortable spot to lie down and nurse its wounds. The wolf's gaze remained fixed on Dumisai while it licked the blood off of its white coat. Dumisai hesitated for a moment before approaching the animal. He had heard talk about white wolves before, but never had he seen one. He was taken by the sheer beauty of the animal covered with its thick white fur and its steely black eyes, even though its fur was dirty and matted with blood. He knew the wolf needed his help but wanted to make sure it was safe before approaching the animal.

"Hello wolf, my name is Dumisai…," the boy offered hesitantly as he attempted to determine if the animal was capable of communicating with him. "You are injured. I can help if you allow me to come closer."

"I know who you are, man-child," the wolf responded while rising to its feet. *"You are the one who possesses the Gift. Many have been awaiting your coming. It is I who was sent to help you."* The animal's voice was distinctly male yet reassuring.

"I am glad that you came. You probably just saved my life, but now you are the one who needs help."

"No need, Dumisai. It is only a flesh wound and will soon heal on its own."

"But what about the rabies sickness, doesn't that need…?"

"It is alright, Dumisai. I am immune to such infections. Save your powers for when they are truly needed. Your compassion is appreciated, though."

Dumisai thought the wolf's advice sounded reasonable and consented. "You said that you were sent—who sent you?" Dumisai questioned.

"One from among your village summoned me. I believe you already know who it was."

"Who?" Dumisai interrogated further. "Was it the old woman?"

"Yes Dumisai, but let's not lose track of what is important here. The heavens have invested in you the Gift, and I am here to help you on your journey in any way that I can. You have within you now the ability to change the course of events unfolding on this plane of existence. You are the one who can point the earth on a new path."

"Yes—I have been told that it is my destiny."

"You have been well prepared then. You will need all that you have learned and more. And now that you have set out to begin this most important work, you must be sure to exercise caution, for the work that you have to do is very perilous."

"Is that why I was attacked?"

"Yes, Dumisai, that was one manifestation."

"Why is the work so dangerous?"

"Do not discount the importance of what has to be done, Dumisai. What you have to do in this lifetime will threaten the very power that currently reigns in this world."

"But that is what I do not understand—why would anyone want me to fail if what I need to accomplish will benefit everyone?" Dumisai asked.

"Not just anyone, Dumisai—the Wanga is a force of evil that has been loosed in the world by men who seek to acquire power for their own interest. It will stop at nothing to keep things the way they are."

Dumisai pondered what the wolf had said and concluded that the extra company would be nice to have around. "By what name are you called?" he queried, satisfied with the wolf's answers to his many questions.

"Unlike with humans, names do not carry much significance in the animal kingdom, but because I understand your human sensibilities, you may call me Áfu if you wish."

"Okay, glad to have you along, Áfu."

Satisfied that the wolf could be helpful to him on his journey, Dumisai resumed his trek to the top of Lookout Point with Áfu walking closely at his side. They arrived at their immediate destination atop the hill and looked down across the valley below, eyeing the town of Milling along the distant horizon. Dumisai looked over at Áfu as if he was expecting to get some last minute advice from the animal. Áfu sat down on his rear haunches offering a glance back toward the boy but remained silent. Dumisai turned his attention toward the town, then he and the wolf began their descent down into the valley together. They both knew that a long walk was ahead of them.

9: The Cave Peril

Dumisai led Áfu down into the valley as he attempted to locate a trail that had already been made by various animals in the area. Sensing Dumisai's intention, Áfu trotted to the front, his action signaling to the boy that he should follow. Dumisai quickly realized that Áfu's natural instinct and sharpened senses could prove to be very useful during their journey. After successfully locating a trail through the underbrush, Áfu waited for Dumisai to catch up before continuing. The path that he found soon led them to a small stream which, after years of water erosion, had managed to cut a deep gorge through the rocks as it made its way down into the valley. The two paused for a short break by the stream, using the opportunity to enjoy a quick drink. Dumisai decided to follow the stream as far as it was practical to do so. He wanted to stay as close to the water as possible as long as it did not cause him to go off of his intended path toward Milling. As they approached near the bottom of the valley, the once gentle stream was becoming noticeably wider and deeper. Looking ahead, Dumisai could see that the path of the stream was being blocked by a large rock formation. The rocks had trapped several sticks and debris that had accumulated over time, resulting in the formation of a small, natural dam which caused the water to collect in a crater and create a small pool. On the other side of the rock formation beyond the pool, Dumisai could hear what sounded like a faint roar. Though the noise seemed to be off in the distance, the persistence of its continuous, uninterrupted rumble was intriguing. With Áfu by his side, he decided to investigate and followed the noise around the edge of the big rock. There they saw the small pool overflowing and transforming itself into a beautiful little waterfall cascading down the side of the hill and collecting at the bottom of the valley into a miniature pond. Dumisai and Áfu carefully made their way to the bottom of the hill. Once they arrived, the boy walked along the edge of the pond while being careful to avoid falling in as he approached the site of the cascading falls overflowing from above. Despite the size, Dumisai still appreciated the beauty that the waterfall had to offer. Its waters sparkled brilliantly, shimmering in the light of the sun. He watched as it overflowed from the top of the drinking pool above, each drop a combination of water and light engaged in an exotic dance all the way down to the bottom of the falls before finally erupting into a spectacular splash of dazzling beauty and grace. Dumisai peered into the falling stream of water, entranced by the beautiful spectacle before finally noticing that the hill over which it flowed had managed to conceal a partially hidden opening. The opening was perfectly situated behind the miniature waterfall, as if it was using the steady downpour to camouflage its existence. Dumisai looked through the wall of water, intent on confirming the existence of something there worth investigating. After a focused stare, he became convinced that the water was indeed hiding an entrance into the hillside. He was careful to avoid the splash of the water as he skillfully approached the entrance, continuing until he was finally close enough to see that it was some type of cave. Dumisai knew that it was potentially dangerous to enter but was curious as to what might be inside. Cautiously, he stepped into the mouth of the cave. He could feel the dampness of the air encountering him at the entrance. The darkness inside made it difficult to see very far in front of him. He glanced back at Áfu as if he was seeking some display of approval from the animal. The wolf had been watching the entire episode but remained hesitant about approaching. Dumisai took a couple more steps into the opening, nearly causing Áfu to lose sight of him. The wolf reluctantly approached the cave opening, attempting to maintain visual contact with the boy. Dumisai proceeded cautiously. He turned and motioned for Áfu to follow, but the wolf had become visibly uneasy. The animal scratched and whimpered before sitting on his haunches with his ears raised alertly. Dumisai watched as Áfu continued his strange, fidgety behavior but was unable to make sense of the animal's actions. Seeing the wolf's uneasiness, Dumisai finally abandoned his stealth and stepped back out of the shadows before turning his attention back to Áfu.

"Áfu…" Dumisai called, "what's wrong?"

The wolf's response was only more agitation. His whimper became louder and more persistent as his behavior became more restless. Dumisai was puzzled but ignored the animal's behavior as he stepped back into the cave. His continued progress into the cave caused Áfu to become frantic. The wolf began to pace nervously around the cave entrance, obviously bothered by the boy's action. As Dumisai took another step into the darkness of the cave, the wolf gave out a low howl. The boy immediately stopped and looked toward the wolf again. Áfu was poised to attack, staring directly into the cave beyond the boy. The hair on the back of his neck bristled as he pulled his ears back in preparation to attack. The apparent danger detected by the wolf seemed more imminent now. Áfu offered a warning in the form of a low growl while peering into the darkness behind Dumisai, flexing his body into a crouched position. The wolf's behavior finally caused Dumisai to stop and reconsider his action. He slowly began backing out of the cave while watching for any sudden movements. Before he could complete his retreat, he felt something suddenly tighten around his ankle, followed by a sudden jerk which caused him to fall onto his back. Áfu sprang from his crouched stance as the boy began disappearing into the cave.

"Help!" Dumisai shouted, "Áfu, help me!"

Áfu lunged quickly, snagging Dumisai's pants sleeve with his teeth, but the strength of the force pulling the boy into the cave caused his pants to rip. Dumisai disappeared completely from sight as he was dragged deeper into the darkness.

It was cold and dark inside the subterranean cavity. Dumisai struggled to regain his footing in the pitch darkness of the cavern as he waited for his eyes to adjust. He stumbled over rock formations protruding out of the ground while trying to get on his feet. Immediately upon standing, he felt a sharp, stinging pain against his lower back. Whirling around, he saw a small, glowing red orb hovering a few feet away. Dumisai stepped in the direction of the object while massaging the spot where he had been hit when he suddenly felt another stinging sensation, this time against the rear portion of his thigh. Dumisai whirled again just in time to briefly catch a glimpse of another red orb as it quickly travelled away from his leg. Before he could react, another orb swooped in glancing him across the chest. Dumisai swatted aimlessly as he attempted to deflect the flying objects. There were several darting around the boy, continuously bombarding him at every available opening as the cumulative effect slowly began to take its toll. Still unable to see anything within the confines of the cave except for the glowing orbs, Dumisai felt his legs begin to buckle beneath him as the orbs became more and more blurred. The last thing he remembered before his body finally crashed to the ground was a silhouetted pair of eyes outlined in red and contrasting sharply against the blackness of the cavernous backdrop. Dumisai wondered if he was dreaming as he lay defenseless on the damp cave floor. His ability to distinguish reality from fantasy finally deserted him, leaving him to watch helplessly as the light slowly faded from view and abandoned him to complete darkness.

Dumisai had no idea how long he had been unconscious. As he slowly opened his eyes, he could barely make out the fuzzy image that was slowly beginning to come into focus. It appeared to be the body of a young boy standing over him. The darkness had receded enough to allow Dumisai to distinguish most of the boy's features in the twilight lighting. Dumisai simply laid there, unsure of what was transpiring. The strange boy continued to stand directly over him as if he was waiting for Dumisai to make a move. Once Dumisai's vision came into full focus, he sat up slowly in order to get a clear view of his surroundings. As he returned his attention to the stranger, he was shocked to see someone who could have easily passed for his identical twin standing directly in front of him. The twin let out an eerie laugh as he observed Dumisai's reaction. Dumisai scrambled backwards on his hands and feet, attempting to place some distance between himself and the mysterious boy. The twin grinned sinisterly as he slowly approached the frightened child. Dumisai quickly tried to stand but the stranger pushed him back to the ground while letting out another menacing laugh. He seemed to be toying with Dumisai, almost as if he was trying to provoke the boy to take some action. Unsure what to do next, Dumisai sat and waited, hoping to buy enough time to plot his next move. His procrastination was short-lived. The twin stood over him glaring menacingly before finally using his foot to push Dumisai back onto the ground. Slowly, the twin bent forward, pressing his face almost directly against Dumisai's as though it was daring the African boy to retaliate. Dumisai retreated in fear. He could feel the wall of the cave directly behind him, cutting off any hope of escape. As he cowered against the cave wall, Dumisai noticed that the stranger-twin seemed to be growing larger. The twin's eyes flashed bright red as its mouth twisted into an even more sinister grin. Dumisai thought he could actually feel evil emanating from it as it towered over him. It was as though the twin-like creature was feeding off of Dumisai's fear. Finally, it reached out in an attempt to place both of its hands around Dumisai's neck. Dumisai's heart pounded heavy in his chest as he futilely attempted to deflect the obtruder's hands. The anticipation of the pressure tightening around his neck caused Dumisai to panic. He shut his eyes as he braced himself for his inevitable demise. Nothing happened. Perplexed, Dumisai opened his eyes. He was surprised to find that he could still breathe freely even though the creature was attempting to squeeze his neck. Dumisai didn't understand what was happening at first, but finally caught a glimpse of creature's face. The once evil grin had been replaced by a look of surprise. Dumisai could still see the hands and forearms of the twin-creature flexing as though they were attempting to squeeze the life out of him, yet he did not feel anything. As he struggled to regain his composure, he suddenly noticed a light emanating from his body. The radiant light seemed to be protecting him from the force being exerted by his attacker. Try as it might, the twin-creature was not able to penetrate the protective aura, allowing Dumisai the opportunity to relax some of the tension in his body and exhale a sigh of relief. Immediately, the boy noticed that the creature's body had decreased in size, indicating an apparent connection between his fear and the thing's power. As the body of the creature returned to its normal size, the aura around Dumisai continued to expand, startling the assailant and causing it to retreat. It attempted to shield its eyes from the ever increasing brilliance of the light and staggered backward, trying to avoid the expanding aura that was beginning to illuminate the entire cave. The light engulfed the twin-creature's body, imprisoning it in a circle of white radiance. Slowly, Dumisai rose to his feet, careful not to take his eyes off of the creature's suspended form. After examining it in detail, he slowly extended his hand toward the entrapped foe. Dumisai tried touching the twin, but his hand did not stop when pressed against its physical form. There was no resistance as his fist breached the chest cavity of his creature's frame. It remained suspended in shock as Dumisai slowly began retracting his fingers from inside of its chest. As he retrieved his hand, Dumisai held a black, gooey blob in his palm. The twin-creature looked on in horror at the blob that was supposed to be its heart. Finally, small, bright red orbs began exiting its form, disappearing into the darkness as they quickly floated away, abandoning the body that they had once inhabited. The twin's physical form appeared healthier now and was able to move within the aura illuminating the cave. Dumisai could see a faint bluish glow radiating from the body of the twin. The twin smiled as he took a step closer to Dumisai. The two boys moved in unison toward each other until their bodies finally merged into one.

Dumisai finally emerged from the mouth of the cave and collapsed to his knees exhausted. He spotted Áfu just beyond the opening but still struggled to maintain consciousness. The wolf tugged at his pants leg in an attempt to pull his dazed body away from the cave's entrance. As Dumisai sat up, he was finally able to shake free of the funk that had come over him following the surreal experience. Áfu positioned its body directly between the boy and the cave to allow Dumisai an opportunity to fully recover.

"Áfu… what happened?" he asked while somewhat still groggy.

"Wanga," Áfu affirmed.

"How do you know that?"

"Isn't it obvious, Dumisai? You were attacked by an evil force not of this world. What else could it be?"

"I guess you're right," Dumisai admitted while climbing to his feet. "I just wasn't expecting that."

"That is why you must be on your guard at all times. The Wanga's strategy is to attack when you least expect it."

"Well, I will be sure to be more careful from now on."

"Good, Dumisai. It is important that you do not underestimate the forces of evil that exist. They sometimes move on the inner planes beyond the detection of the naked eye, but that does not make them any less dangerous. You must maintain your vigilance if you want to avoid placing yourself in harm's way. I'm here to help but there is only so much I can do."

"Is that why didn't you answer when I called out to you?" Dumisai asked.

"I did try to warn you against going into the cave, Dumisai, but our ability to communicate was blocked. It appears that the intent was to ensure that I did not stop you. By choosing to enter the cave, you were placed at the mercy of the dark forces that had gathered there. It is only because of the good within you that you were able to escape this time. Next time you may not be so fortunate."

"I'm sorry for being so careless. I was just curious."

"It is understandable, Dumisai. You allowed external beauty to lull you into a false sense of security. Now you see how looks can be deceiving and outer beauty can mask a thing's true nature."

"Yes, but how can I know when a thing's beauty is not a trap?"

"Use your reasoning ability, Dumisai, and do not rely solely on your senses. Evil is not always so easily detectable."

"If the evil cannot be detected, how can I know for certain where it exists?" Dumisai asked.

"Evil can exist anywhere except where there is love. Usually, evil manifests through the emotions of man. It feeds off of hate, fear, anger, greed and lust. Until mankind comes together in oneness, you will find it wherever you find man."

"But there were no men in the cave," Dumisai countered.

"True, but remember, you are dealing with spirit, Dumisai. Man may be given to being controlled by his emotions, but that

does not mean that his physical presence is always required for evil to manifest."

"If that's true then there is no place that is safe from the *Wanga.*"

"I'm afraid you're right, Dumisai. There is no place where you can hide from evil, but if you hold on to what is true and right, you needn't worry about hiding because your actions will protect you. The important thing is to not get distracted from your goals; the work that has to be done is too important. Remember, you pose a threat to the power that currently rules on this earth and those who are in power will stop at nothing to keep things the way they are."

Dumisai felt ashamed. Maybe the ancestors had made a mistake by choosing him to possess the *Gift.* He wondered if he had jeopardized the trust that they had placed in him by allowing his curiosity to expose him to danger. Sensing Dumisai's thoughts, Áfu brushed against the boy to reassure him.

"Don't be so hard on yourself Dumisai. Even though you have been initiated into manhood, you are young and it is expected that you will make mistakes. Your error was not in following your curiosity; it was in not exercising more caution."

"I will be more careful next time," Dumisai assured.

"I know you will, Dumisai," the wolf replied as it prepared to continue along the shore of the river. *"Perhaps that is the lesson that you needed to learn."*

Dumisai contemplated the words that the wolf had shared as he followed close behind the animal. He tried focusing on other thoughts, but his disappointment in himself persisted. After walking for over an hour, he was still lost in his thoughts when he finally remembered that he had not yet eaten. As Dumisai retrieved some of the fruit that was packed away in his bag, he found a comfortable spot to take a break. He took the moment to observe Áfu as the wolf carefully stalked a rabbit that was scurrying around in the bushes. He had watched animals in the wild catch and eat their prey before, but had never really given much thought to the act. Now that he had witnessed many of them come together without expressing any concern or interest in each other, it was difficult to accept the fact that some animals preyed on others in order to survive. As Dumisai watched Áfu capture the rabbit, the image of blood mixing with saliva mesmerized him. The sight forced him to face the reality of survival for so many creatures in the wild. As Áfu finally finished devouring the meal, he left only those scraps that would be finished off by ants or scavenger beetles. Dumisai was disheartened by what he had witnessed but knew that Áfu had to eat. In an attempt to reconcile his feelings about the action, he reminded himself that this was nature's design and necessary to maintain the earth's delicate balance. Dumisai was glad when Áfu finally exited the woods. He preferred not to think about the predator-prey relationship that existed in nature and quickly shifted his attention to more pleasant thoughts as they continued on their journey.

They walked for two hours before they came to a clearing which Dumisai deemed suitable for setting up a campsite. The setting sun had painted the western horizon a picturesque pastel orange. Dumisai chose a spot next to the edge of the woods and away from the river to pitch the camp. He unpacked the sleeping bag that his mother had so meticulously rolled up for him and laid out a pallet that would serve as his bedding for the evening. He then collected all the necessary items required to build a small campfire. After digging a hole just large enough to contain the fire, Dumisai selectively arranged the firewood so that the kindling wood would be properly placed beneath the larger sticks. Once he was satisfied that he could maintain a reasonable-sized blaze throughout the night, the boy settled in with Áfu curled up close enough to the fire to benefit from its warmth.

Dumisai stared into the star filled sky, replaying the events of the day in his head. Even with Áfu by his side he felt lonely. He remembered how secure he always felt when he was in the comforting arms of his mother, but wondered if such thoughts were even appropriate since he had now gone through initiation. He finally cleared his mind of all extraneous thoughts and hoped to get some restful sleep, but the night shadows continued to spark his imagination. As the shadows rekindled his memory of the creature from his nightmare, Dumisai tried desperately to stay brave. A sudden noise in the woods seemed to purposely test his resolve. He strained in the direction of the noise which sounded as if it was coming from the bushes a short distance away, but the darkness revealed nothing. Even though his immediate surroundings were visible on the moonlit night, the light cast by the celestial body did not sufficiently illuminate the woods in front of him beyond a few feet. He reached for a stick to defend himself as he braced for the unknown. Dumisai listened intently for the next sound to indicate where he should be watching, but now all he could hear was a faint stirring of the wind. As he tried to relax again, the wind picked up slightly, just enough to fan the flames of the campfire. He lay back down with the stick next to him and closed his eyes with the hope that the morning would soon arrive. No sooner had his eyelids shut than he thought he heard what sounded like the wind whispering something to him. He sat up again as fear began to creep back into his thoughts. He looked around futilely, unable to penetrate the surrounding darkness. The wind whispered again. Dumisai was not sure if he was imagining it, but the voice sounded distinctly familiar.

"Grandmother...?" he whispered in response.

"Stay Strong, Dumisai," the voice comforted. ***"Hold on to what you have learned. As long as you follow your heart, you will not fail. Rest now, for you have much work to do."***

Dumisai thought back to the day when he first received the *Gift* and remembered how the wind had spoken to him then. The voice of his grandmother serenading his ears in the form of a gentle breeze was comforting. The wind-song gently chased away any fear that he was experiencing. He looked over at Áfu but the wolf had been sleeping peacefully throughout the entire episode. Dumisai could appreciate the simple wisdom in the animal's example and closed his eyes for the evening.

The next morning they both rose early. Dumisai packed up his camping utensils in preparation to continue towards the city. After taking a drink of water, he and Áfu set out again on their journey. Dumisai chose to break the night-long fast with some fruit that his mother had packed. Reaching into his bag, he located two apples that he deemed suitable. Áfu was already out in front investigating every scent that he came across which could prove to be a potential meal. After satisfying their appetites, the two walked for the remainder of the day until finally approaching the outskirts of the town called Milling.

10: A Different World

Billowing plumes of thick, black smoke spewed from smokestacks dotting the Milling skyline. Dumisai and Áfu could smell the pollution even before they reached the perimeter of the manufacturing town. As they approached the edge of the industrial area, Dumisai began to sense a subtle change in the air. Something about the place made him uneasy. His apprehension seemed born of something inspired by more than mere smog polluting the atmosphere. He could almost feel the impalpable energy as it materialized into the light, greasy film that settled onto his skin. As he looked across the skyline at the gray haze blanketing the town, Dumisai had to make a conscious effort to resist an urge to allow doubts to creep back into his thoughts. The effort reminded him of why he had come to the town in the first place and also provided some much-needed motivation. Dumisai slowly exhaled a breath, giving his eyes an opportunity to completely scan the dismal landscape in front of him. After taking a moment to mentally prepare himself for the task, Dumisai signaled to Áfu that they should enter the industrial town.

Dumisai and Áfu approached the edge of the town's business district just as dusk was beginning to set in. He appreciated the fact that it was beginning to get dark because he and Áfu had already gotten a couple of distant stares from some of the locals. With the night approaching, he turned his attention to finding a place to rest for the evening while also keeping the wolf out of the public's view. Before they were totally enveloped in darkness, he spotted the town's lumberyard and was able to sneak in with Áfu undetected. Even though he had managed to locate a safe place for the night, he knew they would have to leave early the next morning in order to avoid the workers who would be returning to their job. Dumisai quickly found a spot in the shadows close by an exit just in case he and Áfu needed to get out quickly, and settled in for the night.

Áfu was resting peacefully curled up on the ground while Dumisai struggled to get a sufficient amount of sleep. The boy was intimately aware that he could not afford to lose track of the time, and his fear of oversleeping kept him tossing and turning throughout much of the night. Before sunrise the next day, he got up and quickly grabbed his bags as he called out to Áfu in order to wake him. The stars were still out and no early risers had yet arrived at the lumberyard. Not quite sure what to do with his wolf companion, Dumisai headed into the heart of town with the animal close by his side. He hoped to get there early enough in order to find a spot for Áfu before sunrise so that the wolf would be able to wait there undetected.

When Dumisai arrived in the town-center, he and Áfu found themselves nearly surrounded by a mix of wood and brick buildings. All of the buildings were neatly constructed, borrowing from an old western motif and arranged for convenient public access. Dumisai read the wording on the signs of the different buildings. His mother had taught him to read at an early age but he still did not know what the majority of the buildings were used for. One building in particular that caught his interest was the Milling Courthouse. Dumisai remembered hearing his parents remark that the courthouse was the place where "White people" decided on issues of right and wrong. If he was going to make a difference, he figured that this building was as good a place to start as any.

The problem with what to do about Áfu while in the town remained. Dumisai looked around to see if there was anything which he might be able to use to hide his companion. He noticed a bar and restaurant about three buildings down. The restaurant was styled in the tradition of an old-western saloon and was constructed on a raised wooden floor supported by cinderblocks. Planks of timber covered the front and sides of the building, but enough space existed for Áfu to slip through. Dumisai could hardly believe his good fortune. The space under the raised floor of the building would make a perfect hiding place for Áfu while he went about his business inside the courthouse. After making sure that no one was watching, Dumisai quickly instructed the wolf to wait out of sight beneath the building before he walked away to avoid drawing attention to the area.

As the sun slowly ascended the horizon, the town's people began trickling into the various shops and buildings. Dumisai waited until he noticed that a few people had disappeared into the courthouse before deciding to enter himself. He was unsure what to expect as he timidly approached the steps of the building. When he reached the top of the steps and slowly cracked open the door to peek inside, the heavy wooden door creaked loudly, causing everyone in the courtroom to turn and look. Dumisai saw that several people had already entered the building without his knowledge. Recognizing that everyone was waiting for him to complete his entrance, Dumisai stepped through the double doors while still holding the attention of everyone present. He thought that he had interrupted an important meeting because only adults were in attendance. They were all gathered around an older gentleman who was dressed in a black robe and sitting behind a podium in an elevated section at the other end of the courthouse. Dumisai was proceeding slowly up the aisle to the front of the building when a member of the group spoke out in a loud voice stopping him in his tracks about halfway from his destination.

"May we help you?"

"Yes," Dumisai answered, "I'm sorry for interrupting, but I need to speak to someone in charge."

"I am Judge Stone and I'm the person in charge in this courtroom," the man said, broadcasting his words in a loud but non-threatening manner. The Judge's voice sounded distinctly nasal in tone and left Dumisai feeling that he must have irritated the man with his unannounced presence. "Have a seat young man; we will tend to you shortly."

Dumisai took a few more steps forward and quickly decided that he was close enough to the front. He located a seat where he could wait for the conversation between the people to conclude. After several minutes, Dumisai noticed that the group was finally beginning to disperse. Each member of the group took the opportunity to exchange a hug with a young woman before finally stepping aside. Once the meeting ended, Dumisai noticed how everyone appeared to be in a somber mood as they watched the woman push a baby stroller toward the building's exit. He managed to catch a glimpse of the woman's face as she walked past him. Her cheeks were tear-stained, causing him to wonder if he had interrupted some matter of grave importance. Before he could return his attention to the group gathered at the front of the building, he was suddenly startled by the Judge's booming voice.

"Come closer, son. We're not going to bite you," Judge Stone said in a semi-serious tone.

Dumisai moved closer as he was instructed. The Judge leaned forward in his seat while glaring at the boy, his face almost completely expressionless. "Now son, what is it that you want?"

"My name is Dumisai...," he paused searching for the right words.

"Well, boy, spit it out," the Judge responded hurriedly, unconcerned about the boy's nervousness.

Realizing that there was no easy way to state what needed to be said, Dumisai nervously continued. "My name is Dumisai and I've come here to help..." Dumisai paused again as he realized how awkward his statement must have sounded to those listening.

"Well we don't have any work around here, son," the Judge bellowed slightly agitated, attempting to fill in where the boy had left off. "Try one of the restaurants; they may need some help washing dishes or something."

"No, you don't understand," Dumisai replied back, "I've come to help this town... to stop the people here from hurting the earth."

Everyone remaining in the courtroom who heard the exchange immediately stopped in their tracks. Initially, most of the people in the courtroom had a puzzled look on their face as they first looked around at each other and then at the boy. Finally the entire congregation burst into a hearty laughter. Even Judge Stone had a constrained grin on his face. "Okay son, you've had your fun, now run along back home. We have important work to do here."

Dumisai was puzzled by the response. He wasn't quite sure what to do but decided not to move. "Sir, don't you see what is happening? There are things that the people in this town are doing that are hurtful to the earth."

The Judge was starting to get irritated by the boy whom he thought was carrying a childhood prank too far. "Young man, this has gone far enough. I do not have time for anymore of your childish games. This is a court of law and we have work to do here. Run along, now, before you get yourself in trouble!"

Dumisai did not move.

"Bailiff?!" the Judge called out angrily after seeing that the boy was not leaving. "Where's the bailiff when you need him…? Will someone get this boy out of here?!"

The bailiff was waiting just outside the court chamber for the start of his morning shift but quickly set aside his coffee upon hearing the Judge and began to move toward the boy. Dumisai's frustration was evident as he lowered his head in despair. These people did not even take him seriously, he thought to himself. How could he make them understand? Oblivious to the approaching bailiff, the boy turned to walk out of the building hoping to find someone more receptive elsewhere. Before he could make his way to the exit, a young, well-dressed man approached him in the aisle. The man blocked Dumisai's path as he smiled down on the boy in an attempt to reassure him. "Hi, my name is Samuel Goodman," the man said in as friendly a tone as he could muster. "I work in this building. I'm an attorney—ah... I mean lawyer."

Dumisai was not familiar with either term and simply remained silent. The lawyer extended his hand indicating that he wanted to shake. Dumisai looked at the outstretched hand, not exactly sure what the gesture meant. The lawyer withdrew his hand and bent over placing his hands upon his knees in an attempt to convey a friendlier posture.

"And what's your name?" he asked, hoping that he had not frightened the boy with his awkward introduction.

"Dumisai."

"Dumisai... hmm... now that is a very nice sounding name, I don't think I've heard that before around these parts," the man responded, attempting to gain some of the boy's trust. "You know, sometimes grownups can really act like jerks. But I'd really like to hear what you have to say, that is, if you don't mind telling me."

The lawyer's approach was effective. Dumisai was beginning to feel better about the situation after hearing those words come from an adult, and offered a guarded half-smile. Samuel Goodman was a skilled lawyer and knew how to read facial expressions. He instinctively seized upon the moment to inquire further. "How would you like to go outside and discuss this matter over an ice-cream cone?"

Dumisai's expression did not change. He didn't know what an ice-cream conc was, but was glad that he had found someone with whom he could share his concerns. Perhaps this man could direct him to where he needed to go, he thought, if it turned out that the courthouse was not the right place. Dumisai and the lawyer walked outside the courthouse together and headed in the direction of the restaurant where Áfu was hiding. As they walked up the steps of the raised building, Dumisai glanced under the steps, attempting to verify Áfu's presence through an opening in the planks. He didn't see the wolf but continued walking to avoid drawing unnecessary attention to what he was doing. Upon entering the restaurant, Samuel purchased two chocolate ice-cream cones.

"You're not allergic to chocolate, are you?" he mentioned while handing one of the cones over to the boy. Dumisai instinctively raised it to his nose and sniffed, then after first observing the lawyer, he began to lick the ice cream. The rich, sweet taste of the chocolate ice-cream caught the boy completely by surprise; he had never before experienced such a treat. Surely something that tasted so good could not be good for you, he thought. Watching the boy's reaction, Samuel became even more intrigued. He remembered what Dumisai had said earlier in the courthouse and wondered if he should take the boy's story more seriously. His first instinct was to ask Dumisai about why he had come to Milling but didn't want to risk alienating the boy. He knew that the best chance of getting Dumisai to talk freely was to get him to trust the people of the community.

"Dumisai, I'm sorry that your experience here so far hasn't turned out so great."

"It's okay," Dumisai responded. "I'll just have to try again."

"You know, Dumisai, there really are a lot of good folks in this town. Most of the people here are pretty friendly despite what happened back in that courtroom."

"Do you think people are willing to change?" Dumisai asked.

"Yes, change is always possible," Samuel responded, a little surprised by the question. "But change can also be difficult for some people, especially if they already have other pressing things on their mind."

"What kinda things?" Dumisai inquired between licks.

"You know—real life things..." Samuel paused as he contemplated the direction of the conversation. "Dumisai, remember the lady with the baby back at the courthouse?"

"Yes."

"Well, that's a good example of what I mean. On top of everything else that's going on, that lady has a really sick baby to attend to. Those are the kinds of things that people tend to worry about. They're not really thinking about change—just surviving."

"So, something *is* wrong with the baby!" Dumisai said excitedly, as if a long held suspicion had been confirmed.

Samuel was surprised by Dumisai's reaction to the mention of the baby. "Yes, she is very ill," he continued, slightly bemused.

"I'm sorry to hear that," Dumisai replied.

"No, I'm sorry, Dumisai. I didn't mean to sidetrack our conversation," Samuel said apologetically, thinking he could get the conversation back on track. "I was only trying to make a point."

"No, it's okay. Maybe I can help."

Samuel could see that Dumisai was really interested in talking about the baby, and decided to accommodate him. "I doubt it, Dumisai, the doctors have tried everything they know to do, and so far *nothing* seems to help. They're not even sure what's wrong."

"Do you think it will get better?"

"I sure hope so, but nothing's certain. Last I heard, they said that she may only have a couple more weeks to live. It's really a sad situation."

"Wow... I'm sorry. I didn't mean to add to anyone's problems when I came here."

"Well, it's not your fault, Dumisai. Life doesn't stop just because difficulties arise. There are just certain things in life that are important and have to be attended to." Samuel paused a moment to catch his breath before continuing. "Anyway, I was really just trying to give you an idea of why some folk act the way they do. I didn't want you to get the wrong impression about the people here, Dumisai. Normally, we're not all that bad," he added with a smile.

"It's okay, I understand. Do you think I should come back on another day?"

"Well first, why don't you tell me what it is you're trying to accomplish—maybe I can help you."

Dumisai hesitated as he considered the man's offer.

"Dumisai, remember what you said to the Judge," Samuel continued, sensing the boy's uncertainty, "were you telling him the truth?"

"Yes sir," he replied as he took his final bite of the chocolate cone. "I came here to help."

"To help do what, Dumisai? Why do we need your help?"

Dumisai was feeling more at ease now. He had wanted to find someone whom he felt comfortable sharing his story with, yet he knew that it would be difficult trying to convince anyone of the events which had led him to the town. He paused briefly as he reminded himself that he should not trust anyone outside of his village with the knowledge that he possessed the *Gift*. "Sir, do you think that the earth is in trouble of being destroyed by the actions of humans?" he asked after finishing up the ice-cream.

"No need to call me sir, Dumisai. We're buddies right? You can call me Sam."

"But… isn't that disrespectful?" Dumisai protested.

Sam was a little surprised by the boy's insistence. "No, not if I say it's okay. Sam is fine. I promise."

"Okay, I guess, if you're sure," Dumisai agreed reluctantly.

"Yes, I'm sure—now, to answer your question, yes I do think that we humans need to be a little more aware of the consequences of our actions. Sometimes people tend to get so focused on trying to make a living that they… well, *we* do things that may not be so good for the earth."

"But if we don't take care of the earth, we are only hurting ourselves," Dumisai countered.

"Yeah, that's true, but if things get messed up bad enough then maybe we'll finally learn the lesson. At least, then we'll be forced to do something about it. Unfortunately, most people just don't worry about it until it affects them personally."

"Shouldn't someone let them know that it is affecting them?"

"People do know, Dumisai, they just don't care enough to do things differently. That's why we have laws to protect us from ourselves. So, in a sense, we do try to do something about it—it's just that it may not be enough."

Dumisai looked out of the closest window at the grayish hue covering the sky. "It isn't enough."

"Hey Dumisai, aren't you a little young to be worried about all this serious stuff?" Sam asked, hoping to gain some personal insight about the boy. "You know, most kids your age are out somewhere playing baseball or something."

Dumisai was unfazed by the question. His idea of playing usually consisted of spending time in the woods surrounded by nature. "It's very important that I speak to someone who will make the people be more respectful of nature."

"Whoa, you are serious, aren't you? But do you realize how difficult that will be? The steel and lumber industry in this town is pretty powerful. Are you sure that you want to try to convince...?"

POW!—A sudden loud noise which sounded like a gunshot rang out, interrupting the conversation before Sam could finish his sentence. The lawyer quickly jumped up and ran to look out of the window to see what was happening while instructing Dumisai to stay put. A crowd had gathered in the town-center in front of the restaurant where some of the people were pointing toward the building. Sam poked his head out the door hoping to glean some information from the gathering. "What's going on?"

"There's a wolf under that building there," someone in the crowd yelled.

"Yeah, and it must be a *mad* one to have come all the way into town like this," someone else bellowed.

"Wolf!?" Sam called back in disbelief.

Dumisai heard the word and immediately bolted out of the door of the shop.

"Stop! Don't hurt him!" Dumisai shouted as he ran down the steps toward the opening in the wooden planks covering the space beneath the building.

"What tha Sam Hill—somebody grab that boy before he git his fool-self bitten!" the crowd's leader yelled.

"No, leave me alone!" Dumisai yelled back before desperately shifting his attention back to the animal.

"Áfu! Áfu…! Are you okay?"

The wolf approached the front of the building from inside the covered structure and licked Dumisai's outstretched hand that was extended through the planks. The boy was careful to obstruct the view from the crowd with his body so that no one would attempt to shoot the animal. As Áfu forced his body through the wooden planks, Dumisai hugged the wolf while still attempting to protect him as best he could. The crowd stared in disbelief as the boy and wolf greeted each other like they were long lost companions seeing each other again for the first time in many years. Sam had been watching from the restaurant steps and decided to approach. As he took his initial steps, he noticed blood streaming from the animal's side. The crowd had grown even bigger now, as word of the incident quickly spread through the shops in the area. Dumisai turned to face the crowd while still clutching Áfu in an attempt to console the animal.

"Please—he won't hurt you," Dumisai explained. "Please don't hurt him anymore."

Dumisai returned his attention to the wolf again as the crowd began to mumble softly. His concentration was focused solely on Áfu as he placed his hand on the animal's wound, leaving it there until it began to glow with a soft, bluish-white light which expanded to engulf them both. After several seconds, the incident was complete. There was no longer any trace of blood staining Áfu's fur. The two rose to their feet preparing to leave the stunned crowd when Sam quickly approached them.

"Wow! That was some feat! I knew there was something special about you Dumisai, but I had no idea… how'd you do that?" he asked in amazement. Not really expecting an answer, Sam attempted to calm himself upon realizing that his reaction could jeopardize the trust that he had been trying to build between himself and the boy.

"What are you going to do now?" Sam asked coolly after regaining his composure.

"It's not safe for Áfu to stay here anymore," Dumisai replied nervously, unsure of how the crowd would react. "I will have to find a safe place for him outside of town, then I will try to find someone who will listen to what I have to say."

"Well, if you don't live around here, you and the wolf—what's his name…? Áfu? You both can stay at my place, that is, as long as you can guarantee me that he's safe," Sam stated while pointing to the wolf.

"Yes, he is safe," Dumisai replied, "and thank you, we would like that very much."

"You know, you're going to be the talk of the town," Sam added. "You'll certainly have an easier time getting people to listen to you now. Besides, who can ignore anything you have to say with a big, white wolf by your side?"

11: Dispossessed

Sam quickly cleared his work schedule so that he could help Dumisai with his mission. He knew that if the boy was going to have any hope of voicing his concerns to the people of Milling that they would need to devise a plan. Dumisai agreed. He and Áfu accompanied Sam back to his home so that they could get started. As the two began their brainstorming session, Sam suggested that they take the case before the Town Council. He was sure that they could persuade the council members of the importance of enforcing the environmental laws that had already been passed. Dumisai liked the idea of having an adult accompany him to help convince the people of what needed to be done. They decided to attend the council meeting that was scheduled for later that evening. Once the plan was finalized, Sam took the opportunity to complete some of his own work. As he contemplated his workload, he realized that he would have to leave Dumisai at home while he ran several errands. Dumisai agreed to wait for the lawyer to return rather than try to implement the ideas that had been discussed alone. He found a spot outside the house to wait for Sam. Even with the pollution that was evident all around him, Dumisai still preferred the open air of the outdoors to being stuck inside the house. As he waited patiently for the lawyer, his curiosity began to tug at him, enticing him to explore. After sitting for nearly an hour, Dumisai relented, giving in to the urge that he had to investigate. He began perusing the property with every intention of staying close to the residence, but his outing quickly turned into one of his typical excursions and before long, he was lost in the rhapsody of nature.

Dumisai's trek away from the house led him to a nice, shady spot near a park. The location was not far from the town-center and he figured that he and Áfu would be able to wait there comfortably until Sam returned from his errands. He was thankful that he had finally found someone who understood what he was trying to accomplish, yet he still couldn't help but feel alone in the town. In general, the people seemed to be nice but most were not very friendly. From what he could tell, there was no 'Council of Elders' that oversaw the well-being of the entire community, nor did there appear to be the collective sense of community that Dumisai had grown accustomed to. Sam had attempted to explain how the town's government worked, but Dumisai was unable to make sense of the politics. To him, it sounded as though everyone was following mutually agreed upon rules rather than simply following natural law. It was all very confusing. Dumisai was convinced that if he could simply talk to the top rule-maker, then things would not be so complicated, but from what he could gather, there was no such person. At least Sam seemed to know whom they could talk to.

As Dumisai continued to wait patiently in the park with Áfu for Sam's return, he heard the sound of several boisterous voices announcing the arrival of a small group of individuals approaching from a distance. Dumisai counted about six or seven people and all appeared to be older than him, though none were adults. As the group approached, Dumisai stood up to get a better view before finally concluding that the group consisted of all boys who were probably in their early teens. They were loud and unruly, and did not attempt to quiet their voices. As they got closer, it became obvious that they already had a destination in mind. Once they arrived within speaking distance of Dumisai, most of the group finally quieted down, almost as if they were waiting for one among their number to assume the role as their leader. A boy with freckles and reddish-orange hair which was partially covered with an old and worn tam separated himself from his companions by stepping forward to assert his status as the leader of the group. He stopped just a few feet in front of Dumisai while keeping a close eye on the wolf curled up beside the Black boy. After looking Dumisai up and down, the freckled-face boy turned and looked to the others in his group as if he was checking to verify that he still had their support. Satisfied that the situation was firmly in his control, he grinned a suspicious looking smile.

"Well lookey heah ya'll, we done found ourselves a real live, bona-fide colored boy. What yo name, boy?"

"I'm Dumisai."

"Duma-*what?* What kinda crazy fool-sounding name is that?" the group's leader responded while turning again to check for the approval of his companions. Dumisai remained silent.

"Look heah, boy, we don't allow no coloreds 'round heah. Specially no voodoo niggers, so we think you'd be best to git yo stuff and leave while you still can."

Dumisai was surprised by the hostility he detected in the boy's comment. He had heard the word 'nigger' used only once before when his mother had explained to him that it was a term used to demean people of African ancestry. Dumisai warily looked over the entire group and then at his primary antagonist. "I haven't finished what I came here for," Dumisai asserted. "I'll leave when I'm done."

By the calmness in Dumisai's voice, it was obvious that he was not intimidated by the confrontation, yet his reaction only served to further stoke the freckle-faced boy's anger, who misinterpreted Dumisai's confidence as some kind of smug arrogance. The bully took a step closer with his fists tightly clenched, his cocky grin now twisting into undeniable anger. "Boy, you thank we playin' wit you? If you know what's good fo' you, you gon' git gone... NOW!!!"

Dumisai remained puzzled. He didn't understand why the boy had become so angry, but the scowl on the bully's face clearly showed his intentions. Dumisai alertly kept out of the boy's reach by taking a step backward. The other boys making up the group did not intervene, but watched with nervous anticipation. From Dumisai's perspective, their presence was helping to fuel the leader's courage, yet they seemed to be as surprised by the bully's reaction as he himself was. Dumisai's retreat, although minimal, emboldened the bully to press forward. Sensing imminent danger, Áfu rose to his feet. Once standing, the animal's presence immediately garnered the attention of the entire group, causing everyone to stop in their tracks. One of the other boys in the group was clearly afraid of what the wolf might do. He signaled to their leader in an effort to bring the boy back to his senses.

"Billy! Come on man, let's go!" the frightened boy insisted.

Billy looked at Dumisai and then at the wolf again. Áfu's size and growl was a sufficient deterrent for the rest of the group. As they took a couple steps backward, another in the group registered his protest to the red-haired boy. "Billy, let's go man, he ain't worth this!"

Finally acknowledging his peers, Billy pointed to Dumisai as he backed away with the menacing scowl still disfiguring his face. "We ain't finished with you, boy." After what seemed like an endless stare, the bully turned to leave before breaking into a fast trot while the others followed close behind and eventually disappeared into the shadows of the town's buildings.

Dumisai looked at Áfu, hoping to gain some insight into the encounter that he had just experienced. "They did not like me because my skin is different."

"Yes, to them you are different, but you also stirred an emotion of jealousy in them," Áfu explained. *"Since these people now know that there is something different about you, they will most likely deal with you based on their emotions instead of relying on sound judgment. Many of the people here will be afraid of you, and unfortunately, that will determine how they interact with you. It would be better if they did not know so much about you, Dumisai."*

"But I only came here to help," Dumisai admitted.

"That does not matter. The fact that you are different is enough. We must do what we came here to do as quickly as possible and then leave; for I fear that others may come looking to hurt you as well."

Dumisai was definitely not comfortable waiting around for Sam anymore. He knew that he was taking a risk, but decided to go to the Town Hall building alone in order to see what he could accomplish by himself. Besides, Sam had told him that the people would be more likely to listen to him now.

"Áfu, you should wait until I return. It is safer for you, here."

"No Dumisai, I must come with you. We both are safer when we are together."

"Okay, I guess you're right," he agreed.

Dumisai and Áfu walked in the open along the main highway. Most of the people in the town already knew about him and the wolf, so there was no reason to keep a low-profile. They had barely been walking for more than five minutes when Dumisai noticed a shiny red Cadillac slowly rolling along the curb approximately fifty yards back. As he turned to make eye contact with the driver, the car quickly pulled forward, arriving at the curb directly beside Dumisai and Áfu.

"Hey son, that's a fine looking dog you have there," the driver insisted after rolling down his window. "What kind is it?"

"Sir?" Dumisai responded, caught off guard by the question.

"What kind of dog is that there?"

"It's a…" Dumisai hesitated as he remembered the commotion caused by the town's people once they realized that Áfu was a wolf. "His name is Áfu."

"Oh, he's a beaut. Looks like he might be mixed with some wolf though, or something like that."

Dumisai nodded hesitantly, unsure where the conversation was headed.

"Well, look son, my name is Pastor Tidwell," the driver admitted. "I'm the Pastor over at *Milling Church of Christ*, and this here is Dr. Goodwin and that's Deacon Mosley sitting in the back. We saw you walking with your dog and were curious as to what kind it is. If you don't mind, the doctor here would like to take a closer look at it."

"No, thank you," Dumisai declined. "He is fine."

"You sure? I mean, it looks an awful lot like that dog that got shot earlier today. And it was hurt pretty bad too. Dr. Goodwin just wanted to take quick look, son, you know, make sure that he is alright."

As the pastor spoke, attempting to win the confidence of the boy, the doctor and deacon exited the car.

"Thank you, sir, but he is okay now," Dumisai reiterated nervously.

"Aw, c'mon son, we don't mean it no harm, do we Doc?"

"No sir, Pastor," Dr. Goodwin agreed. "We just want to help, that's all."

"See there, son," the Pastor consoled, "we just want to help. Plus, Dr. Goodwin has some ice cream for you. I know you'd like that, wouldn't you?"

"No, thank you."

"What's your name, son?" Pastor Tidwell redirected.

"Dumisai," the boy answered, still unsure of the man's intentions.

"Duma-sigh, hmm...? Okay, well... nice to meet you... umm... Duma-sigh. You know, son, there's been quite a bit of talk about you around town. Did you know that?"

"No, sir."

"Oh sure, why, it seems that you've done some quite extraordinary things since you got here. And you know what else…?" the Pastor continued as he exited the car himself. "It even seems that some of the folks around here are even convinced that you've got some kinda powers. Now, itn't that the darnedest thing you ever heard of?"

"Sir?" Dumisai questioned, his nervousness becoming apparent for everyone to see.

"Oh yeah! I thought it was just some crazy talk at first," the Pastor continued while motioning for the other men to strategically position themselves, "but everybody just kept talking about what happened with that wolf. Well, son, we all know that no one besides God can work outside of natural law. Itn't that right, Deacon?"

"That's right, Pastor," Deacon Mosley agreed.

"Well Deacon, what do you suppose has gotten all the good people of Milling so worked up, then?" Pastor Tidwell asked rhetorically.

"Beats me, Pastor, maybe the boy's done got the devil in'em."

Dumisai listened intently to the exchange but was becoming more uneasy with each passing moment. He began backing away slowly as Áfu turned his ears backward and emitted a low growl while keenly watching the movements of the three men. Pastor Tidwell looked toward Dr. Goodwin and subtly nodded as if he was giving the man a pre-planned signal. Dr. Goodwin quickly reached into his jacket, withdrawing a wadded up fabric made of a thin rope-like texture.

"Áfu, go!" Dumisai yelled as he spied the doctor's sudden movement out of the corner of his eye.

Before either could move, Dr. Goodwin slung the rope-net over Áfu, ensnaring the wolf before he could get away. Dumisai turned quickly, attempting to run away but the two remaining men were quickly upon him before he had the opportunity to escape. As Pastor Tidwell used the weight of his large frame to hold the boy down, Deacon Mosley quickly tied the boy's hands together with rope as a temporary restraint before securing the rest of his body. The three men then tied the net-entangled wolf to a tree before struggling to get Dumisai loaded into the back seat of the car.

"Don't worry, son," Pastor Tidwell advised while pulling the car away from the curb, "we're not gonna hurt you. This is for your own good. Just you wait and see. You'll be thanking us soon enough, you hear?!"

Dumisai wiggled and twisted to no avail while struggling to get free of the binding and ignoring most of what the man was saying. After several minutes of riding, the Cadillac finally pulled into the parking lot of a large building. The three men exited the vehicle with Deacon Mosley dragging the resisting Dumisai out of the back seat. The boy could see a sign that read *Milling Church of Christ* as the deacon and doctor carried him into the church's sanctuary and then laid his body across a large table in front of the church pews. As Dumisai looked around the sanctuary, he noticed the peacefulness that permeated the room. To his left he could view the empty pew seats that waited invitingly for someone to come and let go of their frustrations. To his right, he saw a large "T" shaped carving etched onto a wooden board that separated the floor seating from an elevated section of seating behind a podium and microphone. The figure of a man was carved out of the wood onto the T-shaped fixture, but Dumisai was unsure what it was supposed to represent. Beneath the figurine on the T-shaped Cross read the words: *This Do In Remembrance Of Me.* Dumisai stared at the carving while contemplating the possible meaning of the words before turning his attention back to the pastor. Dr. Goodwin held the boy in place in order to secure him to the table as Pastor Tidwell made the sign of the Cross with his right index finger and recited several Bible verses in preparation for his ritual.

"Heavenly Father," the pastor prayed, "in your holy name, we ask that you grant us the strength of your holy spirit as we attempt to heal this child whose body has been fettered with evil."

Deacon Mosley retrieved a container with water which he passed to the pastor before helping Dr. Goodwin firmly secure Dumisai.

"In the name of Jesus, I beseech you, unclean spirit, to come out of this boy, right now in the holy presence of almighty God!" exclaimed Pastor Tidwell while sprinkling the water over Dumisai with his fingers. "Depart accursed spirit, for God has decreed that this child's body is His rightful dwelling place, and His alone! None but the Father is worthy of taking up residence amongst his children. Depart! I command thee, in Jesus name!"

Pastor Tidwell continued shouting commands consisting of biblical verses in the direction of the restrained boy, clearly working himself into a frenzy as he tried to get a sign that the devil was losing its hold on the boy's body. Still immobilized, Dumisai watched the preacher, perplexed by the frantic words and actions of the man calling on the power of God while directing his angst toward him. He could see the preacher's frustration building with each passing moment that nothing extraordinary occurred. Pastor Tidwell's annoyance was becoming obvious. Dumisai noticed sweat beginning to bead across the man's brow and his eyes starting to outline with red. The preacher was oblivious to everything besides accomplishing his mission, and Dumisai was convinced that the man was beginning to become possessed himself. Even though he had seen rituals where people became possessed, he still watched in astonishment as the pastor entered an entranced state. Sweat was beginning to drip profusely from the preacher as he called on the spiritual assistance needed to accomplish his objective.

"In the name of Jesus, I bind you Satan! Come out of this child, NOW!" Pastor Tidwell exclaimed passionately while slamming his fist down on the table beside the boy.

Dumisai could almost feel the hostility rising in the preacher standing over him. He closed his eyes in an attempt to block out the preacher's biblical rant as Deacon Mosley dabbed the preacher's brow with a handkerchief. Slowly, Dumisai's body began to glow with a soft white light, causing Pastor Tidwell to momentarily pause. The pastor was briefly encouraged, concluding that the exorcism was finally beginning to produce a desirable result. The boy's body began rising slowly off the table, only to be restrained by the rope tied to his wrists and ankles which was securing him to the table's surface. Pastor Tidwell stopped briefly to watch in bewilderment.

The soft glow temporarily disappeared, only to reappear below Dumisai's navel, first radiating outward and then fully encircling his mid-section. Dumisai remained suspended in the air as the glowing light contracted into a single luminous ball which pulsed brightly at its point of origin before contracting again into a small circle of light. The light-circle slowly followed an imaginary line up the center of his body to his navel, sternum, heart and throat, pulsing with energy at each of the locations. Once the light reached his throat, it disappeared again only to re-emerge on his brow just between his eyes. Finally, the glowing light rose from the top of Dumisai's head, radiating brightly as it fanned up and away from the still suspended child. Pastor Tidwell watched in dumbfounded amazement, not sure what to make of the spectacle. As the light continued to rise, it dispersed outward until eventually reaching the ceiling of the church and then passing through it into the waiting atmosphere above. A turtledove sitting atop the church, cooing its soft song paused briefly as the billowing wave of energy saturated it, bathing it in a cocoon of vital energy. Immediately, the dove began to sing excitedly before suddenly flying away, retracing the car's path to the park on the outskirts of the city where Áfu was still entangled and tied to the tree. The wolf instantly recognized Dumisai's life-force emanating from the bird. The subtle force attracted several field mice which arrived out of the woods ready to receive instructions on freeing the entangled wolf. After several minutes, the mice were able to successfully gnaw through the rope, allowing Áfu to finally be free from the entanglement. Without hesitation, the wolf followed the turtledove which flew swiftly back to the church. As they approached the church building, Áfu leapt without breaking his stride, crashing through one of the church's stain-glassed windows. The sudden commotion of shattering glass surprised the men. They immediately turned in the direction of the noise, shocked to see the wolf charging toward them.

"Jesus Christ…!" Pastor Tidwell yelled, shocked by the sudden development. "It's that dang wolf!"

The three men scattered, leaving Dumisai lying bound on the table. Áfu wasn't interested in the frightened men. He trotted towards Dumisai as the men scrambled to exit through a back door leading away from the sanctuary. Dumisai managed to squirm his body to the edge of the table.

"We must hurry," Áfu admonished as he began gnawing at the knot in the rope which was binding the boy's hands. The animal's tugging successfully loosened the knot enough for Dumisai to work his hands free. Dumisai quickly shifted his attention to the rope binding his feet together.

"Let's go, Áfu!" Dumisai announced as he snatched the remaining rope from around his ankles.

Suddenly—*Pop! Pop! Pop!* The small caliber pistol sounded more like a firecracker than it did a handgun.

"Don't hit the boy! Just get that wolf!" Pastor Tidwell reminded as he yelled instructions to the gun wielding deacon.

"Don't worry, Pastor, I'll get'em!"

Dumisai and Áfu darted through the exit at the back of the sanctuary but could hear the men quickly approaching. Dumisai led Áfu into the hall where the church offices were located. At the end of the hall he could see an exit leading outside. The boy and wolf raced to the door only to see the knob turning before Dumisai could reach for the handle. As the door began opening outward, Áfu jumped. The weight of his large body caused the door to swing open forcefully, knocking Dr. Goodwin down the steps and onto the ground.

"There they go!" Deacon Mosley yelled as Dumisai exited through the open door. Pastor Tidwell and Deacon Mosley scurried down to the end of the hall only to find Dr. Goodwin slowly rising to his feet.

"Shucks… let'em go!" Pastor Tidwell relented, attempting to catch his breath between words. "Mayor Suggs won't like it none too much that he got away, but oh well. How much trouble can some kid sniffing around cause anyway?"

"I agree, Pastor," Deacon Mosley admitted. "I never understood what was so dang special about the kid anyway."

"Well, for me, the issue is still the salvation of that boy's soul. And that's the tragedy of this whole thing, Deacon—that poor lad's still got the devil in 'em."

"Amen, Pastor," Deacon Mosley agreed, "amen!"

Dumisai and Áfu headed into the woods just beyond the church cemetery. They did not stop running until they were well into the forest. Áfu led the way through the woods toward the road which led back to the park. Dumisai needed to rest but the sense of urgency was evident. It seemed that the longer he stayed in this town the more bad things continued to happen. Luckily, he was able to find his knapsack that he had been forced to abandon when he was abducted. He retrieved a light snack as he paused to rest prior to heading to the Town Hall building.

12: Consequences

Dumisai and Áfu both walked hurriedly into the heart of the town's business district. Several people stopped and pointed as the boy and wolf made their way toward the Town Hall building. Dumisai was uninterested in the stares that he and Áfu were receiving. He was determined to complete the task that he had initially set out to accomplish by coming to the town, and approached the building without entertaining any thoughts of self-doubt. Although he wanted the people of Milling to understand that he had come there to help, he realized that he would have to be bolder in his approach if he wanted them to take him more seriously. He decided to allow Áfu to accompany him inside of the building in order to avoid any more situations with the town's people. As they both ascended the steps to the Town Council, people who would ordinarily be engaged in their own personal pursuits stopped to watch, trying to figure out exactly what was happening. Dumisai entered the building with the wolf by his side, causing an uproar among the occupants in the hallways. Those who saw the animal quickly darted inside of the nearest office, some swearing and slamming doors as they went. Upon hearing the commotion, the building's security officer quickly rushed to the scene in an attempt to gain control of the situation. In his excitement, he nearly fumbled his gun as he hurriedly removed it from its holster.

"Get that animal outta here!" the officer yelled toward the boy.

The security guard succeeded in getting Dumisai's attention with his shouting.

"It's okay—he won't hurt anyone," Dumisai yelled back down the hallway.

"I know it ain't hurting nobody, cause you fixin' to get it outta here. You hear me!!?"

"Sir, if you just let me speak to someone in charge..." Dumisai replied, hoping to change the focus of the guard's attention as he continued walking in his direction.

The nervous guard aimed his weapon squarely at the animal's head. "Get it out now or I'll shoot it!"

"No! Don't shoot!" Dumisai yelled back, now clearly nervous himself.

"I'm tellin' ya, I'm gonna shoot! I don't like big dogs— they make me nervous!"

Others in the building began to emerge from behind their locked doors and were peering from behind the security guard for protection. The site of the other people encouraged Dumisai a little.

"But it's okay, he won't hurt you!" he responded in a more subdued tone, attempting to calm the guard.

"How do I know that, boy? He don't even look like no dog I ever seen before!"

"That ain't no dog," one of the men peering from behind the security officer interjected with amazement, "that's a wolf...!"

"Wolf?!" the security guard exclaimed incredulously. "What tha Sam Hill you doing with a wolf in this building?!"

Any progress that Dumisai had made toward calming the guard had been completely destroyed. He knew that the mere thought of Áfu being a wolf was alarming the people. He would have to somehow convince everyone present that Áfu was safe so that he would not have to leave the animal alone again. Just then, someone in their haste to get to the safety of an office slammed a door shut in the hallway. The sudden loud noise caused nearly everyone within hearing range to jump including the security guard who, with his already high state of anxiety, unwittingly squeezed the trigger of the weapon that he still had trained on the wolf. The firearm exploded with deadly force as the bullet ripped through the air toward its target. Instinctively, Dumisai raised his hand toward the speeding missile as if he had anticipated the entire sequence of events. The air was momentarily suspended as the bullet speeded along its path before finally losing all of its forward momentum and dropping out of the air just in front of Áfu. There was stunned silence in the halls. The crowd that had gathered behind the security guard looked at the boy in disbelief. They noticed that his hand, which was still outstretched, also had a dim glow surrounding it. The security guard slowly lowered his weapon before allowing it to completely drop to the floor. His mouth was still agape as he stared blankly at Dumisai, unsure how to react to the events that he had just witnessed transpire before his eyes. The sound of the gunshot had caused the crowd of onlookers to swell. Several people began moving toward Dumisai, anticipating an explanation of some kind.

After a moment of seemingly endless silence, Dumisai noticed the incredulous looks on the faces of the people in the hallway. If he was going to state his case, this was the opportune moment.

"My name is Dumisai. I need to speak to someone in charge. Someone who is responsible for making the laws that everyone here lives by. It's very important."

The silence among the crowd slowly evolved into a low mumble.

"The Town Council is scheduled to meet later this afternoon," someone finally shouted from the back of the hall gathering. "Maybe you should wait around to meet with them. I'm sure they will be very interested in hearing what you have to say."

"Can you show me where they meet?" Dumisai asked excitedly, hoping to finally get an opportunity to possibly speak before the council. If it was anything like his own Council of Elders, he figured that he should be able to make some progress toward his goal.

"Sure, I will take you there," voiced a woman of medium build and dark brown, curly hair. She stepped through the crowd in an effort to make her way to the front. The woman was rather dark complexioned, her skin appearing to be tanned. Dumisai recognized a hint of African ancestry in her even though her features were convincingly European. The idea that two people, one Black and the other White, could come together and produce offspring of mixed heritage was still foreign to him, yet seeing her immediately made him feel more comfortable than he had been at any other time while in the town.

As they engaged in conversation, the dialogue between Dumisai and the woman helped to calm the other people present. Many of them began to gather closely around the boy in hopes of gaining some insight into who he was and his presence in Milling.

"Shoot! I say we get those council folks together and have an emergency meeting right now," offered a man in his mid-twenties.

"Yeah, I agree! Most of 'em should be here anyway. I want to hear what this boy's got to say!" someone else admitted.

"Alright then, let's do it! This is important."

The momentum had clearly shifted toward gathering all the necessary people together so that a meeting could be held for Dumisai's benefit, which suited him fine. As the crowd turned and began to move down the hall, the mixed-race lady signaled to Dumisai to follow the group.

"My name is Angela, we're going to try and set that meeting up with the Town Council for you."

"Thank you, I'm Dumisai, and this is my friend Áfu."

Just beyond the detection of the crowd gathered in the hallway, a dark dog-like silhouette slinked into the shadows. Sensing the strange presence, Áfu let out a low whimper.

"What is it, Áfu?" Dumisai queried as he attempted to comfort the wolf by scratching behind his ears.

"Excuse me, people," a man standing near a window interrupted. "It seems that we have a little situation out front."

As the crowd shifted to get a look, Angela again made her way through the gathering.

"Dumisai, you stay here," Angela insisted. "I'll go see what this is about."

Following Angela's lead, the hallway audience pushed through the doorway leading out of the building to the courtyard to confront the assembled mob.

"What's going on here? What do you people want?" Angela demanded.

"Give us the boy!" the mob's leader shouted. "We don't want no trouble, just give us the boy and we'll be on our way."

"Yeah!" several people in the crowd shouted in agreement.

"Now, look," responded Angela, "you know I can't do that. What's this boy done to you—any of you, for that matter? He's just a child."

"That ain't no normal child, Ms. Ward," a voice exclaimed from within the midst of the crowd. "That boy's a pawn of the devil!"

"YEAH!" the crowd roared again.

"Pastor Tidwell?" Angela quipped, somewhat surprised. "I can't believe you're in on this."

"He's right, Ms. Ward," a red-headed teen interjected, "I seen it myself!"

"Billy Hicks, what in the world are *you* doing here?"

"I jus' don't think it's right, Ms. Ward—him comin' here and try'na show us up 'n all."

"Listen, folks," Angela asserted, "you all should just go on home. We'll take care of the boy."

"No, Ms. Ward!" the leader of the group insisted while inching the crowd closer to the building's door. "We ain't leaving without the boy!"

"YEAH!" the crowd roared back in agreement.

Dumisai was clamoring to hear what all the commotion was about. As he strained to get a better angle from which he could view the crowd through the window, he caught a glimpse of a dog-like shadow darting across the end of the hallway. He immediately abandoned his interest in the crowd outside and went to investigate. Dumisai moved quickly in the direction that he had seen the dog's shadow moving against the hall corridor. Áfu emitted a low growl as he slowly followed, keeping the boy within his sight. Dumisai ignored the wolf's warning, determined to satisfy his curiosity. He turned the corner of the hallway and was momentarily frozen by the sight of a dazzling array of dancing red lights apparently awaiting his arrival. The bright reddish-glowing orbs danced frantically through the air, swirling about each other as if in a frenzy. The closer the light circles came to each other, the faster they seemed to churn. Eventually, the smallest circles of light coalesced, forming larger circles. As the light expanded, the lambent orb began to lose its sheen, growing darker and making what had previously been a scarlet red into a shadowy, sanguine mass which was unrecognizable in form. The substance continued to grow while being bombarded by the remaining blood-red orbs until it finally completed its transformation. The result was a fully-formed, black jackal-like creature standing on all fours with the crackle of energy pulsating around it. The energy bubbled conspicuously, outlining the creature in blood-red effervescence. It shot a deathly stare of contempt toward Dumisai as it pulled back its black gums, exposing sharp, white teeth. Its dark red eyes and tongue contrasted sharply against the black mass of energy which appeared to be in constant motion. The creature emitted a visceral growl before suddenly pouncing toward the still startled Dumisai. Instinctively, the boy attempted to elude the quasi-liquid jackal-creature by diving out of the way, but the effort was futile. The force of the impact knocked him onto his back. Dumisai scrambled to regain his footing as he recalled his earlier experience with the *Wanga* in the cave, but the creature was quickly upon him again, forcing his back against the hallway wall. He could feel the viscous nature of the energy bubbling against his brown skin. The dark-reddish glow outlining the creature's form pulsed violently as its eyes searched menacingly for the most appropriate spot to strike. Dumisai searched his peripheral vision for Áfu. He could hear the wolf's forceful attempts to get at the creature even though some unseen force was holding the animal back and preventing him from assisting. Dumisai tried dislodging the jackal-beast from atop his body but the effort was useless; the creature would not budge. It appeared to be toying with him, savoring the final moments before completing a kill. Dumisai knew that he was at the mercy of the creature and searched desperately for anything that could be used as a weapon, but nothing was within his reach. His desperation nearly sent him into a panic as the creature began its final assault, trapping him underneath its tenebrous form. Dumisai's world went dark as he was engulfed in the suffocating swirl of the creature's sepulchral blackness. He opened his eyes, pushing aside the blackness only to find that the air around him had become almost completely suspended. It was as though the world itself had begun moving in slow motion. Dumisai could see a distorted image of Áfu silently fading in and out of view. His ability to distinguish between illusion and reality deserted him as he lost control over all of his mental processes. He was certain that his life was slipping away as he drifted in and out of consciousness. Each pass into the darkness became more inviting than the last. It seemed to be beckoning for him to come in as if it was a genuine place of refuge.

Dumisai wanted to embrace the darkness. It appeared to be somewhere that he could escape from the tumult which was assaulting him.

As Dumisai prepared to accept his fate, he noticed a group of people standing around and silhouetted in light. They seemed to have suddenly materialized out of thin air, appearing initially as an ephemeral haze before coming clearly into view. The sight was sufficient reason to eschew the darkness. Dumisai could see that the people were singing—or maybe chanting, and strained to hear what they were saying. Slowly, the volume increased until the words were finally able to penetrate his enduring stupor and find their way to his ear.

"CHIN----GEL----YEN----GEL----YE."

Their voices were faint and wafted lazily through the air, vocalized in a slow sing-song fashion.

"CHIN---GEL---YEN---GEL---YE."

Dumisai heard it again. It was still faint but more distinct this time.

"CHIN-GEL-YEN-GEL-YE."

As soon as Dumisai recognized the phrase, it triggered something deep within his psyche. His eyelids fluttered forcefully just before he felt his body go completely limp. Immediately, he was plunged into a state of disequilibrium but was left partially aware of his surroundings. In front of him could be seen a narrow tunnel which was illuminated briefly by several intermittent flashes of lightning. The rapid flashes were accompanied by a thunderous rumble that suddenly shattered the deathly silence. Dumisai stared blankly into the tunnel as if he was looking at something that was no longer there. He could feel a sensation of intense heat beginning to rise up in his chest and radiate throughout his body. Suddenly, a jolt of electric current unexpectedly shot through his being, invigorating him with a newfound sense of power. Dumisai enjoyed the upsurge in energy but was surprised by the aggressive nature of it. It felt as though some foreign force was attempting to exert complete control over his body. He quickly realized that he had no control over what he was experiencing even though he was fully aware of everything that was happening. He felt completely displaced from his form as though he was watching himself from a distance. He could see his body radiating a soft, white glow that increased in intensity until it became tinged with a blood-red hue. After several moments, the concentrated glow exploded, discharging a focused blast of light that hurled the jackal-creature violently against the ceiling. The force of the impact caused a large wall painting to come crashing down to the floor where it landed next to the stunned creature. Dumisai continued to watch as the entity that had taken control of his physique ripped a portion of the carpet from the hallway floor, using it to bind the creature's ductile form. By now, the weakening creature exerted very little effort in resisting and appeared to be defeated.

Almost as if on cue, the first of the spectators began to arrive, momentarily distracting Dumisai. Seizing the opportunity, the red light-orbitals that had formed the creature quickly darted away, leaving the crumpled carpet to fall limply to the floor.

"Whoa! What happened here?!" the first man to arrive asked, not believing the damage he was seeing.

Dumisai was whisked away suddenly. It felt as though his mind was breezing through the tunnel of light, racing to merge back with his dislocated body. He blinked three times as if trying to force himself out of a dazed stupor before finally realizing that he was actually standing over the crumpled carpet himself and not simply observing the scene from a distance. Immediately, the look of confidence that had previously adorned his face was replaced by one of bewilderment. As soon as the realization set in that he was back in control of his own body, Dumisai collapsed exhausted. Several of the men rushed to Dumisai's side as he slowly attempted to rise to his feet.

"Are you alright, son?" one of the men asked.

"Y-Yes," Dumisai replied, clearly exhausted even as he attempted to straighten out the carpet and collect the broken pieces of the picture frame. "I'm sorry for the mess, I can work to pay for this."

"Don't worry about that now, son," the man comforted, "the important thing is that you're okay."

"Yes… I'm fine."

"Dumisai!" a voice from the back called as the crowd of people began to swell. "We've got everything calmed… Oh my God!—what in the world happened?!"

Dumisai recognized the face of the woman as she emerged from the crowd. "Ms. Angela… I'm sorry…"

"It's okay, we can deal with this later," Angela instructed. "Right now, we have to go meet with the council members. They've already started gathering in the chamber."

"Wait…," one of the spectators yelled as the crowd exited the hallway, "isn't someone going explain what happened here…??!"

Angela led the crowd to the chamber's entrance where she waited for an official okay to enter the council meeting. As the crowd streamed in from the hallway, the council members watched, searching among the faces for the enigmatic child that they had heard so much talk about. Dumisai and Áfu were at the rear of the group. As they entered, the room fell quiet. After everyone was seated in the chamber, Dumisai was finally directed to the middle of the chamber floor. The town Mayor was an older gentleman and his presence brought to mind the Judge whom Dumisai had faced earlier that same day. After thoroughly looking the boy over, the Mayor spoke: "Well young man, so you're the reason we've had to rearrange our entire agenda for this meeting?" he said facetiously while keeping his attention focused directly on Dumisai.

Dumisai nodded shyly in front of the assemblage that was eyeing him with baited anticipation.

"I understand that you have quite a few talents," the Mayor continued. "Perhaps when we're finished here, you can give us a little demonstration if you don't mind."

Dumisai remained silent, unamused by the comment.

"Well what exactly is it that's so important, that you've been able to get everybody so worked up?"

Before Dumisai could speak, someone approached the Mayor.

"Mayor Suggs, excuse me for interrupting," the man whispered over the chairperson's shoulder, "but you have a call."

"Can't it wait, Roscoe?"

"They said it was important, sir."

"Alright, I'll take it in my office," he relented. "Umm, excuse me ladies and gentlemen of the council. It seems I have an unexpected emergency that I must attend to. Please carry on without me with the other items that are on the agenda, but I want to be here when we discuss this young man."

Mayor Suggs retreated to his office. He was there approximately five minutes before Roscoe poked his head through the door, motioning for him to return. The Mayor held up one finger, indicating that he was nearly done with the call.

"Yes… yes sir," Mayor Suggs insisted as he attempted to wrap up the call. "I understand completely, sir. Yes sir, I'll be sure to remind Judge Stone of his obligations. Thank you for the call, sir."

After hanging up the phone, he rejoined the assembly of people that had been waiting patiently for his return.

"Folks, I apologize for the interruption," Mayor Suggs said as he re-entered the council chamber. "I had to take an important call, but we can continue now. Did we make any progress while I was out?"

"Sir," one of the other council members interjected, "this is the only item on the agenda for today."

"Very well then—let us get started, shall we?" he said, ignoring the point that everything had been held up waiting for him.

Dumisai was still standing at the center of the chamber floor as he waited for someone to signal for him to begin. He looked at Angela for instruction. She nodded her support, reassuring him that it was okay for him to speak. Dumisai panned the room, briefly observing all the curious faces that had gathered to hear what he had to say. Fortunately, he was able to draw upon different situations from his childhood that had prepared him for this moment.

"Sir, thank you for the opportunity to speak before your council. My name is Dumisai. This is my friend Áfu. We have come here because we want the people of this town to know that they are in danger."

"What do you mean, son?" Mayor Suggs asked with confusion in his voice. "What kind of danger?"

"The earth, sir—it is dying because of pollution. The lives of all of us depend on a healthy earth."

"So, that is the danger that you were speaking about—a little pollution?"

"Sir, each day the earth dies a little bit more because so many people do not treat it as a living creature which deserves our care and respect."

"Well, I don't know about that, son. I see life thriving all around us."

"Haven't you noticed that there are hardly any animals here? They've all left this area because everything here is dying."

"Well, to be honest, we have noticed a lot fewer animals around town, but we have laws to address that. You can rest assured that protecting the environment is a top concern for us here in Milling. Heck, one day we might even clean up some of the pollution that can be seen around town."

"That is not enough. Things will only get worse unless a change is made. Don't you see all the smoke that pollutes the sky everyday?" Dumisai reminded, his voice starting to rise, reflecting his increasing confidence.

"Ohh—the smokestacks," the council spokesman stated with a half smile in a moment of revelation. "Son, we are very much aware of the smoke that comes from those stacks. We have guidelines in place to ensure that our processing plants stay within environmental regulations."

"But you said that you have laws to protect the earth," Dumisai retorted, "how can you have laws to protect the earth, yet you allow those factories to continue polluting the air and water?"

"Son, those factories are very important to our economy here in Milling. Many people work there and wouldn't have a job if it weren't for those factories. Besides, our factories perform a tremendous service not only for this town, but also for this country. Many of the things that are made there are used by people all across these United States. We can't just shut them down," he offered calmly, hoping to allay the concerns of the boy with some simple logic.

Dumisai was not satisfied with the answer. He decided to try a different approach and hope for a better result. "What about the river? The water is not suitable to drink because it has also been polluted."

"Yes, we know about the water. We have laws to protect the water from further pollution also, plus I already told you that we have plans to clean up the river someday, but tell me... umm... Du-mi-sai?"

"Yes."

"Son, is this really the reason you're here in Milling? Based on the things I've heard about you today, I thought you were going to share with us some secret wisdom or something."

Several of the people in the chamber were able to detect the sarcasm in Mayor Suggs' voice and laughed softly.

"I came so that you would know the consequences of your actions," Dumisai responded.

"So you came here to tell us about these things that we are already fully aware of and to question our way of life?"

Dumisai was frustrated and remained silent while thinking of the best way to respond. He was sure that he could hear hostility in the Mayor's voice. He did not understand why so many people could not see that he was only trying to help.

"Surely you don't really expect us to shut down our steel and lumber mills because you are upset about a little pollution, do you?" Mayor Suggs continued. "Who did you come here with anyway?" he asked, no longer amused and seemingly annoyed that he had even agreed to accommodate the boy.

"I came alone with my friend Áfu."

"Look, I know that the pollution is a little disturbing to you. Heck, when I was a kid, I was idealistic myself. But you're still a child and we are the adults, son. We know what we're doing. We appreciate your concern about the environment, but we'll take care of things here in Milling. Run along now, you've taken enough of these people's time."

"NO!" Dumisai exclaimed loudly, recalling the similar sentiment that had been expressed by the Judge earlier, "I will not 'run along'! Can't you see what you're doing? Your pollution is hurting the animals here! It's hurting you too, you just don't know it! You have to make the people obey the laws that are there to protect them!"

The entire council membership was surprised by the boy's outburst.

"Boy, how dare you raise your voice at me," Mayor Suggs snapped as he recoiled in anger. He banged his gavel down hard, dismissing the boy's comments and the meeting. "Son, this meeting is adjourned. We will keep in mind your concerns, but right now we have real business to attend to."

Dumisai stood stunned before the assembly with feelings of both shame and disappointment. This was the opportunity that he had come so far for, and it was ending unsuccessfully. As the people began to whisper among themselves, the noise level in the chamber began to rise making it difficult to make out the words of any single person. Dumisai contemplated his next move. He hoped to get everyone's attention one final time so that he could apologize for his disrespectful outburst before leaving the assembly. In the midst of the commotion, Mayor Suggs discreetly motioned to one of the security officers, calling him to his desk before whispering something in his ear. The security officer quickly retrieved his walkie-talkie and began relaying the instructions before descending into the crowd.

Angela pushed through the gathering in an attempt to get to Dumisai so that she could offer him some comfort. As she approached the boy to put her arm around him, people began filing out of the council chamber into the adjoining halls, creating a bustle of activity. Mayor Suggs banged his gavel in an attempt to get the crowd back under control, but to no avail. The chamber floor had already degenerated into a pit a chaos. Everyone was trying to exit the crowded room when Angela saw someone pushing through the hall in an attempt to get to the chamber floor. The person's forceful entry disrupted the general flow of movement out into the halls, causing the crowd to wonder what was happening. It was Sam Goodman. Upon seeing his lawyer friend, Dumisai forgot about his defeat in the council chamber. He waved to Sam, hoping to get the man's attention. Once Sam spotted Dumisai, he maneuvered his way through the crowd to meet the boy.

"Hey Dumisai, I'm sorry it took me so long to get here," Sam said apologetically after finally reaching Dumisai. "How'd it go?"

"Not very good," Dumisai admitted. "I guess I should have waited for you."

"Well, don't be discouraged—we can always try again. We'll just keep trying until they listen to what we have to say, right?!"

"Right," Dumisai agreed with a smile. He was encouraged by Sam's optimism.

"Hi, I'm Angela Ward," Angela interjected at Sam, refusing to be ignored.

"Hi Angela, I'm Sam Goodman. Nice to meet you," Sam answered hurriedly. "Dumisai, you want to see something neat...? Quick—step outside with me for a minute."

Dumisai followed Sam out of the building as Angela and Áfu tried to stay close. As they stepped through the building's doorway, the group was treated to a spectacular sight. Twilight lighting had replaced the late afternoon sunshine of the otherwise typical day.

"Why is it so dark out here?" Dumisai asked. "It's not supposed to be night yet."

"It's a solar eclipse," Sam explained, "but don't look directly at it or you could hurt your eyes!"

Dumisai was careful not to stare directly at the blackened moon-disk which was blocking the light from the sun. The people leaving the Town Hall building seemed mesmerized by the event. They stood watching in awe as an air of discomforting silence began to descend over the crowd.

"I knew something strange was going on here!" a man finally admitted in a voice loud enough for others to hear.

"It's that boy!" Pastor Tidwell exclaimed, allowing superstition to overtake his reasoning ability as he stoked the concerns of the already restless crowd. "I told you that boy's got the devil in him!"

"YEAH!" members of the crowd yelled back in agreement as they began to turn their attention toward Dumisai.

"Now settle down, people," Angela yelled back, trying to keep the crowd under control by appealing to common sense. "It's just an eclipse. It doesn't have anything to do with the boy!"

"Eclipses have always been considered a bad omen!" the first man yelled back to Angela. "Seems mighty strange that we'd have an eclipse on the very same day that kid shows up!"

"People, listen to yourselves!" Angela exhorted. "This isn't the only place in the world where the eclipse can be seen!"

Simple logic seemed ineffective on the crowd. Sam quickly realized that he had inadvertently placed Dumisai in danger and tried to bolster Angela's argument. "People please... this is nothing but silly superstition! You folks know that!"

The crowd was not listening. No amount of reasoning seemed to help. Dumisai seemed oblivious to all the commotion around him as he began making his way to the edge of the steps. His attention appeared to be completely preoccupied by some other phenomenon.

"Dumisai, stay close by me, buddy," Sam reminded as he turned to confirm the boy's whereabouts.

Dumisai had already walked away and was heading directly into the waiting crowd.

"Hey, Dumisai... where you going?!" Sam yelled nearly panicked.

As he hurried to retrieve Dumisai before the boy could reach the steps leading to the crowd, Sam stopped abruptly upon seeing the thing that had captured the boy's attention off in the distance.

"Oh... my... God...!" Sam muttered beneath his breath. His mouth hung open as he looked out and saw a throng of animals, all of which appeared to be converging on the town. The entire herd of animals seemed to heading toward the Town Hall building at an orderly pace. As more people became aware of the sight, the entrancing power of the eclipse seemed to lose its spell-binding hold over the members of the stunned crowd. They looked on in astonishment as various animals descended on the town-center. Dumisai walked down the steps of the building, passing uninhibited through the crowd of onlookers. As he stepped forward to meet the flock of animals, they fanned out in a circular formation almost completely surrounding the boy. The spectators in the crowd were not sure how they should react. People began to amass around the perimeter of the circle of animals, looking for a way to watch whatever happened next.

"Wait!" a woman's voice from among the crowd yelled in desperation. "Please—let me pass... I've got to get through!"

The woman continued to push through the crowd of people that had gathered to watch the spectacle. As people directly in her path recognized her, they stepped aside somewhat befuddled but allowed the woman to pass. Immediately upon reaching the edge of the circle of animals which enclosed Dumisai, a space opened as the animals moved aside, allowing the woman to enter.

"Please… you have to help me!" the woman pleaded as she approached Dumisai.

Dumisai seemed surprised by the woman, unsure why she had come to him.

"Please! I've tried everything else," the exasperated woman continued as she stepped closer. "Please help my baby. Please… I'm begging you. I heard about what you did. You have to help my baby!"

Dumisai could see the desperation on the woman's face as he looked down at the listless body of the baby she was carrying. It appeared to be already dead. "I'm sorry, ma'am—I wish there was something I could do."

"No! Please—you have to do something!" the woman demanded as she extended her hands holding the baby. "You have to try! My baby can't be dead. Please, take her!"

Dumisai took the baby in his arms. Her body was still warm even though there was no pulse that he could detect. He examined the baby closer, but still found no sign of life. If there was any breath or a heartbeat, it was too faint to detect. As he prepared to return the child to its mother, Dumisai noticed that the animals had now completely surrounded him and the woman. He looked around the circle as each animal kneeled on its front legs. The action reminded him of the power that had been entrusted to him. By now the entire population of downtown Milling had gathered to see what would happen as they anxiously anticipated another spectacle. Dumisai pulled the baby close to his chest as he felt an energy beginning to stir among the animals forming the circle. The invisible force strengthened as it flowed between the assembled animals that were kneeling in silence. The energy flowed freely, surging through an invisible electro-magnetic field that connected the animals with the surrounding plant-life before finally shooting through Dumisai himself. He could feel the pulse of their collective force coursing uninhibited through his body, bathing him in a sea of life-energy that saturated every fiber of his being. He felt as though the streaming current of bioelectrical force had immersed him in a torrent of potency, infusing him with power that he was unaware even existed. Almost immediately, the top of his head began to glow with a bluish-white aura which moved slowly down his shoulders until it completely encircled him. The glow expanded, eventually connecting with the black stone that he wore around his neck and causing it to emit a bright blue light that contrasted sharply with the soft glow that had engulfed the boy and baby. The onyx stone suddenly emitted a brilliant beam of light that shot up into the atmosphere before spreading out into divergent bands, interspersing throughout the crowd and finally sweeping through the entire town as separate streams of ancestral energies. Instinctively, Dumisai raised the baby skyward as the glow that surrounded him continued to pulse brightly. After a moment of absolute stillness, the baby shuddered abruptly and then began to squirm before letting out a loud cry. Immediately, a roaring cheer erupted among the crowd of onlookers. Dumisai gently handed the sobbing child back to its mother whose eyes had already filled with tears.

"Oh, thank you, thank you, thank you! Thank you so much!" the woman said gratefully while wiping the streaming tears from her cheek. "Oh, my baby... you saved my baby. Thank you so much!"

Dumisai returned a smile that seemed to express some measure of satisfaction as the aura slowly began to fade from his body and the stone talisman. Each animal began rising to its feet before turning to depart from the town in the same direction that it had come. As the circle opened, Dumisai felt a brief jolt as the beam of light suddenly returned, re-entering the black onyx stone of his necklace. The resultant flash of light shocked the crowd out of the apparent spell that had overtaken them, finally allowing the people an opportunity to process everything that had occurred.

"Mommy, look!" a small boy exclaimed. "The eclipse is over!"

"Hey, he's right!" a man replied after turning his attention skyward. "With all the excitement, I had completely forgotten about it!"

A low rumble began to slowly engulf the crowd as the realization set in that the sky had become completely free of smog. Even the idle smokestacks which towered above the town's industrial quarter off in the distance seemed out of place against the backdrop of the clear, pristine skies. Everyone marveled at how clean everything had become. The thick, heavy energy hanging over the air had completely dispersed as if some tremendous burden had been lifted from the town and its people. As the people began to realize the significance of everything that had happened they hugged each other as if a moment of clear revelation had finally descended upon them. Both Sam and Angela raced toward Dumisai who still remained standing in the same spot. Once they reached him they were both eager to ask many questions, but aware that he may be exhausted, they only put their arms around him for support.

"Dumisai, are you all right?" Sam asked.

"Yes, I am fine."

"Wow, that was amazing!" Angela exclaimed. "How'd you do that?"

"I only did what needed to be done," Dumisai admitted. "I can't really explain how."

"Look, there he is!" someone yelled excitedly as the last of the departing animals left Dumisai in plain view of the waiting crowd. "He saved the baby!"

"Let's hear it for Dumisai!" another man shouted before leading everyone in a series of excited cheers.

The festive atmosphere continued for more than thirty minutes as the people of the town continued to celebrate the accomplishment. Angela was amazed at how quickly the very same people that had wanted to condemn Dumisai only minutes earlier were now cheering him. She was glad that the crowd had decided to embrace him, but knew that she and Sam still had to remain vigilant in case certain attitudes shifted again. Eventually, the crowd began to thin out, leaving several people still milling around the area. Angela and Sam tried to use the opportunity to get Dumisai away from the scene without drawing any more attention to themselves, but was suddenly interrupted.

"Impressive," Judge Stone confessed as he approached the three of them before they could get away, "if I do say so myself."

"Oh, Judge Stone," Sam responded surprised, "we didn't see you coming."

"Oh, yes, I saw the whole thing."

"Your honor," Angela interrupted, "with all due respect, sir, we'd like to take Dumisai home to get some rest. This has been very taxing day for him."

"Yes, of course—I just wanted to tell the lad 'thank you'. That was my granddaughter you just saved, son, and

I want you to know that I truly appreciate what you did. If there's anything I can do for you, just let me know."

Sam looked at Dumisai, letting him know that he should take advantage of the moment to speak.

"Sir," Dumisai began, "I only wanted to let the people of this town know that the animals, like each of you, are a part of God's creation and have a right to inherit an earth that is healthy and whole. All of the pollution threatens that, not only for the animals, but for everyone here."

"Your point is well taken, son," Judge Stone agreed. "I will do all that I can to see that some changes are made. I don't make the laws but I will throw my weight around a little, if you know what I mean."

"Thank you," Sam offered on Dumisai's behalf.

"No, thank you!" Judge Stone countered as he extended his hand toward Dumisai. "I'm the one who owes the debt of gratitude here."

Sam remembered that Dumisai was unfamiliar with the gesture and shook the Judge's hand in his stead. "Thanks, Your Honor, we'll make sure to hold you to that."

"Well, good day, folks," the Judge offered before blending into the remnants of the crowd that was still waiting to disperse.

"What happens now?" Angela asked.

"There is nothing else that I can do here," the boy responded. "It is up to the people to make their own choices."

Dumisai signaled to Áfu as the three began to make their way out of the remaining crowd. None of them saw the police officers that were approaching.

"Sir… Ma'am…we'll take it from here," the Sheriff interrupted.

"Excuse me, officer?" Sam responded, surprised to see the group of policemen. "What's the problem here?"

"I'm Sheriff Cummings and we have orders to take the boy with us."

"Whose orders, if you don't mind me asking?"

"We're not at liberty to say that, sir."

"Well, is he under arrest?!! Where's your warrant?!!"

"Sir, we don't have a warrant, but again…"

"No…! No way, Sheriff!" Sam interrupted angrily. "I'm a lawyer and you're not taking this child anywhere. He is going with me. Come back once you have your papers in order!"

"Sir, are you sure you want to do this?"

"Oh yes, Sheriff! I've never been more sure of anything in my life! If you don't want the Police Department sued into oblivion, you'd best get your act together before you come trying to haul an innocent child away!"

"Very well—have it your way, sir," the Sheriff replied, acknowledging a temporary setback before turning to his deputies. "Guys, let's go."

"What was that all about?" Angela asked, confused.

"I don't know, but I don't like the way things are starting to play out. Let's get out of here while we still have the chance!"

Not understanding what was happening, Dumisai looked to both Sam and Angela as they all began to walk slowly away from the scene.

"Thank you both for all your help. You helped me accomplish what I came to do despite everything that happened."

"Dumisai…," Sam responded, "you have truly made an impact on the people of this town. I think I can speak on behalf of most everyone when I say that your coming here will definitely affect the choices that the people make going forward."

"That's right, Dumisai," Angela agreed. "We have all been blessed by your presence."

"Thank you," Dumisai replied. "Now that our work here is done, Áfu and I will be leaving soon to return to my village."

"Dumisai," Angela offered, "you know where to find us if you ever need anything."

"Yes, thank you. I would like to rest now, it has been a long day."

13: Dreamscape

Dumisai tried unsuccessfully to hide the embarrassment he felt as he scarfed down the food that had been provided to him. He had already eaten a full serving but his appetite was still not sated. As he finished the remaining portion of the meal on his plate, he looked over at Angela to make sure that it was okay to help himself to another serving. Angela smiled, letting the boy know that it was fine. She and Sam were enjoying watching Dumisai and Áfu satisfy their appetites, and were happy that their guests had gotten the opportunity to enjoy a full course meal prior to their departure. After he finally finished eating, Dumisai thanked his hosts for their hospitality and then excused himself from the table. He wanted to take some time to relax while his food digested before gathering his belongings in preparation for the long trip home. Angela packed several extra items into his bags. She wanted to make sure that his return trip would be as comfortable as possible, especially since he had insisted on walking.

Dumisai was eager to get started on the long walk back through the wilderness. He regretted having to leave his new friends but knew that the time had come to depart.

As he said his final goodbye, he gave Sam and Angela each a long embrace. Angela wiped away a tear as she released the boy from her hug and wondered what would become of him. Dumisai smiled as though he could read her thoughts and then signaled to Áfu that the time had come to begin their journey back to the village.

As Dumisai made his way along the edge of the woods, he recognized the hill that he and the villagers had come to know as Lookout Point off in the distance. The familiar landmark was a welcomed sight and he was glad that his journey was finally coming to an end. The journey had taken a toll on him physically, plus he was emotionally drained and looking forward to sleeping in his bed again. As the evening pushed further into the night, he observed the dark, overcast sky above. It was devoid of stars, and grayish clouds completely blocked out the light from the moon, making for a dark and dreary evening. It was nearly impossible to determine how late it was, but Dumisai was sure that it was well past the time that most villagers would be up and about. The trill lullaby of a whippoorwill trailed ominously through the trees as a distant rumbling of thunder suggested that rain might also be on the way. A slight wind picked up as if to emphasize the possibility of rainfall. With the threat of inclement weather hanging over his head, Dumisai decided to seek shelter for the evening rather than make a nighttime push up the rugged terrain of the hill. In case he needed further incentive, a flash of lightning briefly lit up the evening sky as larger than normal raindrops began pouring down.

The din of rain beating against the forest canopy created a cacophony of dissonant sound. Dumisai quickly found a cluster of trees that could be used as temporary shelter from the downpour. Within the span of a few minutes, the rain suddenly stopped as abruptly as it had begun, providing him with an opportunity to construct a quick lean-to which could serve as shelter for the evening. After completing the task, he was satisfied that he and Áfu could at least remain dry through the night, and was appreciative of the fact that they should easily be home by the middle of the next day.

Áfu curled up close to Dumisai as the two tried to settle in for the evening. An occasional clap of thunder served as a reminder that the rainy weather might not be over. While lying under his cover, Dumisai noticed that the forest was unusually quiet. He hadn't noticed the silence before, but now that it had come to his attention, the quietness seemed eerily unnatural. He listened intently for a few moments, straining to hear the chirp of some crickets or the croak of a frog, yet the eerie silence was absolute. Dumisai tried to put it out of his mind as he rolled onto his side, attempting to get comfortable enough to fall asleep. Any investigation would have to wait until tomorrow. Another wave of rain soon came, causing the sound of the steady downpour beating against the top of his makeshift shelter to drone noisily in his ears. The monotonous din proved to be strangely relaxing and helped induce a deep and lucid slumber, providing Dumisai with some much needed rest from his long journey.

A crack of thunder boomed violently, shaking the air immediately surrounding Dumisai and suddenly shocking his consciousness back to a state of awareness. He had no idea how long he had been asleep, but the bombastic thunderclap caused him to sit up on his pallet wide-eyed, even though he was still groggy. He needed a moment to get his bearings. There was a jumble of images still fresh in his mind as he struggled to determine exactly where he was at. He checked his surroundings which seemed familiar, yet couldn't quite place his exact whereabouts. As he looked around, there was no sign of Áfu, just some items scattered about which he was unable to make out in the dimly lit space. As his eyesight began to adjust to the lighting, he slowly started to recognize some of the items which were located along the walls of a room that he found himself in. There were gourds and clay pots which triggered a sense of familiarity, as did the flat divination baskets and the strong, dank odor which permeated the air. The smell was so recognizable that he was sure he had been there before. After noticing various masks placed strategically around the room and a string of gourds connected by a rope, he finally remembered where he had experienced the unforgettable odor before. He was back in Ol' Manzalele's hut. Dumisai looked around slowly, trying to understand how he had arrived back at the location. He had no recollection of returning to the village, and certainly not any of going to the old woman's hut. He heard a loud noise in the adjacent room that caught his attention. Dumisai stood to his feet and carefully made his way across the floor to investigate. The door to the room was closed but the noise inside seemed to be getting louder by the moment.

"Hello…?" Dumisai called out nervously as he slowly approached the door. "Who's there…? Ms. Manzalele… is that you?"

There was no answer. The commotion sounded as though it was intensifying. Dumisai slowly cracked open the door to peek inside but was met by an overwhelming force which knocked him back to the floor. The door swung open wide and Dumisai was able to see an impressive display of light energy exploding before his eyes. He could sense the distinct presence of evil in the room while slowly climbing to his feet, but instead of fleeing, he was drawn to the scene like a magnet. He returned to the doorway and watched the light display for nearly a minute before finally deciding to enter into the luminous maelstrom. Instantly, Dumisai found himself observing an epic battle playing out in front of him. A woman resembling Manzalele, except much younger, was dressed in purple and red garments, and was confronting a single shadowy figure. From a distance the shadowy being appeared to be a man except that it had no face. It was agile and moved with swift execution. As fast as it was though, the woman appeared to always be a step ahead of it. Dumisai marveled at the fluidity of her movements as she wielded a spear in her off hand while reacting to the attack mounted against her by the faceless creature. She stood straight but nimbly dodged several light blasts consisting of red and black hues aimed at her from the fingertips of the shadowy perpetrator. A thrust from her spear missed its mark as the shadow-being eluded by acrobatically using a high-flying somersault. It underestimated the woman's agility, however, and landed squarely on the point of her lance. Instantly, two more faceless beings entered from the shadows, replacing the vanquished victim. One attacked from the rear as the other aimed a forceful burst of light directly at the front of the woman's head. She instinctively cart-wheeled out of harm's way, leaving the creature that was attacking her from the rear exposed to the deadly blast. Two additional creatures quickly replaced its lifeless body as it fell to the floor. They attacked in unison, attempting to catch the woman unprepared. She easily out-maneuvered their attack by drawing the villainous horde toward her and then gently pushing forward with her open hand, dispersing them with an invisible force that seemed to defy the simple movement witnessed by Dumisai. Without hesitation, the woman continued her onslaught, tearing through the faceless creatures, only to have two more take the place of every one that had fallen. She noticed that with each creature she destroyed came an increase in her power, but still the sheer number of the beings was becoming too much to handle. Rather than destroy any more and increase the total number confronting her, she retrieved a white powder from a bag slung over her shoulder and sprinkled it around the perimeter of her body as a bulwark of protection. She then began casting another powdery substance in the direction of the creatures. The powder magically bound them, rendering them all harmless without destroying them. Recognizing what was happening, the remaining free creatures briefly retreated. The reprieve was short-lived, however, for they began calling upon all of the evil forces within the reach of their influence.

Dumisai watched as what appeared to be wild and crazed animals began collecting around the woman. They were foaming at the mouth with glaring red eyes and distorted features. The woman was completely surrounded by what appeared to be an unending legion of evil. Neither victory nor escape seemed possible. Rather than succumb to the throng of evil, the woman turned and locked her eyes onto Dumisai while slowly retrieving some herbs from her bag. Without hesitation, she placed the herbs to her lips, her gaze still fixed on the boy. Immediately, her body fell to the ground. Within moments, a wispy mist rose from her crumpled form. Dumisai was seeing it with his own eyes, but he didn't understand what was happening. The spirit-like mist headed directly toward him, causing every natural instinct within his body to scream for him to move out of its path, yet he couldn't. It entered his body, causing him to stagger backwards in an attempt to retain his balance. He felt an instant surge of energy travel through his body as the woman's life-force coursed up his spine, causing a brilliant flash of light to shoot skyward, immediately attracting the attention of the entire legion of creatures. Even though his presence had been previously unknown to them, the sudden surge in power had made it impossible for him to remain unnoticed. The creatures turned immediately, attempting to locate the source of the light-burst as they made preparation to attack anything willing to be host to the woman's life-energy. They moved swiftly in the direction of the light, led blindly by their hatred for their former nemesis. As they honed in on the energy source, they reached the doorway where Dumisai had been waiting concealed from view. To his surprise, the creatures began screaming in agony as their eyes came upon him. He looked down at his body and noticed that it was glowing bright white. The luminous brilliance of his aura was unbearable for the creatures to look at. Their agonizing wails continued unabated until their screams finally shocked Dumisai back to a state of wakefulness, causing him to sit up abruptly in the makeshift shelter.

Now that he was awake, he felt amazingly powerful and rejuvenated. He could feel the energy still coursing through his body as images began to rush in uncontrollably. His mind became flooded with memories that he did not recognize. Images of Manzalele intermingled with images from his own past. He recognized visions from her childhood years that flashed briefly into his consciousness. The experience was overwhelming, resulting in too much information for him to process at one time. Dumisai was unable to distinguish his own thoughts from those that belonged to the old woman. He wondered if he was going insane as he struggled to regain control over the images that were streaming into his mind, pushing him to the brink of madness. As the swirl of images deteriorated into a blur, Dumisai felt himself slipping into darkness and buried his head in his hands.

"FOCUS, DUMISAI." He recognized the voice as belonging to Manzalele. *"IT IS UP TO YOU NOW, EH?"*

The words were like a splash of cold water across his face, riveting Dumisai back into the immediate reality of the moment. He quickly gathered his wits, turning just in time to see Áfu staring transfixed at the moon. The animal appeared to be somewhat anxious, as if it was expecting something to happen. Suddenly, Dumisai felt the source of energy exit from his body, carrying with it all the disjointed memories and depleting him of the additional strength that he had briefly enjoyed. The sudden deficiency left him momentarily dazed. He struggled to clear his head as he tried to regain his composure. He saw Áfu's body flash with a bright blue aura before the animal suddenly sat on his rear haunches and let out a howl. Then everything was quiet again. Dumisai seemed spooked by the eerie silence. Finally, the hoot of an owl broke the seeming silence of the night, refocusing Dumisai's attention on his surroundings. He noticed that the rain had passed, leaving only the intermittent drip of water splashing off the cover of his shelter.

Day was about to break as the first blush of sunlight began to penetrate the trees of the forest. The incessant sound of frogs croaking had returned, mixing with the serenading songs of various birds and restoring the pre-dawn air to a state of normalcy. Dumisai gathered his belongings while waiting for the sun to complete its overnight journey to the top of the eastern horizon. He could hardly wait for the morning to arrive as he prepared to resume his journey home so that he could be amongst the people of the village again.

14: Homecoming

Upon reaching the top of Lookout Point, Dumisai looked out over the valley and was barely able to distinguish the Milling skyline from the distant horizon. As he marveled at the distance he had traveled, he recalled his journey and the people he had met. He hoped to return one day and find that his intervention had made a lasting impact on the town.

"Well done, Dumisai," Áfu offered, realizing that the end of their journey was imminent. *"You are well on your way toward accomplishing what you came to earth to do. Just stay focused on why you are here and you will surely be successful."*

Dumisai turned to acknowledge the animal but Áfu was gone. The wolf's disappearance was as mysterious and sudden as had been its arrival. Dumisai knew that the reason the wolf had come in the first place was to offer guidance and protection while he was on his journey, and now that he was safely within a couple hours of home, Áfu's job was finished. Dumisai had grown emotionally attached to the wolf and was saddened by its departure, but he knew that he could not expect the animal to abandon its natural lifestyle to stay with him. As he replayed the animal's final words in his head, he wondered if their paths would ever cross again. Looking around one last time, Dumisai eyed the outskirts of the village settlement before resuming his trip. After finally making his way into the heart of the village, some children who were out playing stared curiously at him as though they were trying to figure out why in the world some stranger would bother to come there. Looking closer, a young girl recognized Dumisai and began running towards the boy's hut.

"DUMISAI….! Dumisai's back!"

The girl kept running and yelling as people began emerging from their huts to see what was happening. Dumisai's mother was the first adult to see the boy. She ran toward her son, fighting to control her emotions. Their embrace was long and firm.

"Oh Dumisai, my little man, I am so glad that you are home," she cooed while squeezing her son tightly. Malaika stepped back arms length from Dumisai, inspecting him from head to toe. "How are you doing, baby? Have you eaten anything? Come inside and I'll fix you something! Are you okay? Come on and sit down, I know you must be tired. What do you want to eat, baby?"

"Malaika, he's not a baby anymore," Bento reminded as he pushed through the group of interested spectators that had begun to form.

"Mom, I'm fine. I missed you too. How are you doing? How's everyone?"

"Oh, we are doing just fine," Malaika continued, trying to remain cognizant of her son's status. "Come on in now and rest while I fix you something to eat."

A small crowd had already gathered around Dumisai and his mother.

"Dumisai, welcome home, son," Bento interjected as he hugged his son.

From the back of the gathering, Baba Kenje was able to maneuver his way to the front and looked the boy up and down before displaying a slight smile.

"So you have returned," the old man said triumphantly. "We knew you would come back to us. And victorious too, I'm sure! You'll have to tell us about your journey!"

"Yes, Baba," Dumisai agreed. "But first I'd like to speak to the old woman... Ms. Manzalele—I want to tell her about the dream that I had."

"Dumisai," Baba Kenje replied, the excitement in his voice trailing off, "I'm afraid I have some bad news, son. Manzalele passed last night."

Dumisai gasped when he heard the news, recalling the events of his dream-like experience.

"What happened, Baba?"

"She must have passed in her sleep, Dumisai. We found her this morning in her bed. Come to think of it, we never really saw too much of her while you were gone. But last evening she mentioned that her time among us was almost done, so naturally we went to check on her when we didn't see her out and about this morning. I must say that she did appear to have made a peaceful transition though, because she died with a smile on her lips."

The thought of Manzalele smiling seemed so far removed from all the memories that Dumisai could conjure in his mind. His recollection of her as the stern elder was etched firmly into his memory.

"Now that she has made her transition," Baba Kenje continued, "the council will take up the issue of her burial."

Baba Kenje exhaled a big breath as he briefly recalled the life of service rendered by 'Ol Manzalele.

"But enough about that now, son," he resumed, "you need to get you some rest. And we've got plans to make if we're going to celebrate your return, right!?"

"Yes sir," Dumisai concurred, allowing himself a smile as he embraced the feeling of pride that the people of the village were expressing toward him.

"Excuse me, Bento. I didn't mean to impose on your reunion with your son," Baba Kenje offered apologetically.

"No need to apologize, Kenje," Bento insisted, "we appreciate all that you do for us. It's no imposition at all."

"People, let's leave this family to their privacy," Baba Kenje admonished before turning to leave himself. Following the old man's lead, the crowd slowly dispersed allowing Dumisai and his parents an opportunity to reunite in private.

An air of excitement sifted through the village, building in anticipation of the coming enstoolment ceremony for the departed Manzalele. After three days of mourning, most of the villagers were eager to assist with the ancestor veneration ritual. With so much excitement in the air, the occasion seemed more appropriately suited for offering a tribute than it did for performing a funerary service. Ritual drummers awaited their cue to kick-start the ceremony using the evocative power of the drum. Once the call was sounded, they began drumming with unbridled passion, beating out syncopated rhythms at such a frenetic pace that the crowd was quickly transformed from a mass of idle bystanders into a throng of passionate participants. The air became electric with a ritualistic resonance. The smell of cypress and sage saturated the stillness of the early afternoon air. The combination of sound and scent seemed to conspire in an effort to transport the participants away from the normalcy of day-to-day village life to a world reserved for communing with spirits.

The affair continued for nearly thirty minutes. The period proved to be sufficient enough time for the majority of the people to succumb to a ritual-induced state of trance. Women trained in spirit possession swooned in delirium, captivating the onlookers and plunging the participants into an even deeper trance-state. As the ritual reached its apex, the women, in their altered state of consciousness, began exhorting luminous ancestors to come and greet the spirit of the deceased elder so that she could be accepted into their sacred realm. They chanted incessantly until some of the women appeared to be overtaken by an unseen force. The women staggered back and forth, muttering unintelligible words while attempting to maintain their footing as the possession took complete control of their bodies. Several elders gathered around the possessed women in order to receive counsel from them. The villagers joined in, empowered by the exchange of energy being generated by the ceremony, dancing and adding their energy to the festive mix. Baba Kenje and selected elders carefully guided the process, making sure that the ritual was being conducted in a manner that was consistent with the traditions and customs that they had brought with them from Angola. In addition to ensuring that Manzalele received the proper assistance once she awakened as an ancestor in the inner planes, the elders wanted to use the ceremony as an opportunity to teach ritual protocol to the younger generation.

Dumisai watched the events with keen interest, attempting to gain as much understanding from the ceremony as possible. How fitting, he thought, that 'Ol Manzalele was still imparting the wisdom of the ancestors even at her own funerary ceremony. Even as he recalled his memories of the old woman, he could not shake the feeling that he had not seen the last of her. After all, hadn't it been her who had made a point of teaching him that energy could assume various forms? He knew that death of the physical body was not the end, but rather a transition, especially if one had lived an honorable life. And everyone was in agreement that Manzalele's life was certainly worthy of honor. Most of the villagers had never had any real interaction with the old woman directly, but all were aware of the selfless life of service that she had rendered to the community. All that remained was to follow proper protocol to ensure that her spirit would be accepted into the ranks of the honored ancestors.

Once the enstoolment portion of the ceremony concluded, the feast which traditionally marked the occasion of all major celebrations was already set to begin. Most of the people had worked up a hearty appetite because they had intentionally refrained from eating earlier to avoid having a full stomach interfere with their ability to go into trance during the ritual. The sharing of food amongst villagers was a way to strengthen the communal bond between the people. The fact that the feast could also be used to celebrate Dumisai's return home proved to be a matter of good planning. The majority of the food had been prepared prior to the ceremony, leaving the villagers free to socialize while waiting for it to be served.

The entire village was still giddy from the ritual energy which hung over the air like a thick fog. People hurried to change into their finest traditional garments, hoping to take full advantage of the exuberance of energy. Before long, crowds were mixing freely as they gathered in obedience to the call of the enticing rhythms beat out on the cylindrical, conga-like *Ngoma* drums.

Dumisai sat quietly while enjoying the festivities and partaking in the meal which had been prepared. He hadn't realized how much he appreciated the sense of camaraderie on display among the people in the village. It was good to be home again, he thought as he sat engrossed in the festivities of the ceremony, only occasionally remembering to take a bite of his food. The relaxing nature of the music, dance, and ritualistic atmosphere were sure to help him settle back into the normalcy of village life. The celebration lasted well into the evening as the people partied into the night.

Exhausted from the activities of the day, Dumisai finally excused himself from the festivities to head back to his parent's hut. He had walked nearly halfway home, leaving the bonfire and the accompanying noise of the celebration behind when he noticed a group of magpies perched high in a tree directly in front of him. The outline of the birds' black and white bodies with their long tails were clearly distinguishable against the backdrop of the full moon. Dumisai thought it was strange to see the birds at such a late hour, but even more so that a group of three would be there together. He stopped to observe them briefly, allowing the magpies an opportunity to look him over before finally flying off. Dumisai quickly dismissed the sighting as just an odd occurrence and resumed walking toward his destination. He had barely moved when he noticed someone standing in his path a short distance ahead. The person stood in the shadows cast off the trees by the moonlight, making it difficult for Dumisai to make out who it was. He could see that it was someone short in stature and standing with their head bowed while leaning on a wooden staff for support. Dumisai approached slowly, curious about the identity of the late-night dweller while waiting for them to offer a greeting. As he stepped directly in front of the person, she slowly raised her head, revealing the milky-pale complexion of her skin.

"Manzalele…?" Dumisai was stunned and only managed to mumble the woman's name under his breath.

"Come with me," the woman demanded before turning to walk into the nearby woods.

Dumisai obeyed. The woman's voice sounded hollow and distant, but it still commanded the usual authority over him. He knew he had just recently witnessed the woman's burial, but he could not bring himself to disobey her instruction. Manzalele remained silent for the duration of the trip, never once checking to make sure that Dumisai was following. She arrived at the clearing in the woods by the large magical tree with the gaping hole at the base. The area was illuminated by the full moon which loomed imposingly over the forest clearing. Dumisai could see several people standing on the perimeter of the open space with their backs turned toward him, while others were seated just inside the circular clearing with drums. Everyone in attendance seemed to be waiting in anticipation of the start of some event. Most of the people present were wearing an *Akishi* mask except for a few women who were close by. Manzalele motioned for Dumisai to come into the center of the clearing and wait.

The boy obeyed as the drummers began to beat out a soft rhythm which gradually increased in volume and fervor. The drumming slowly intensified, eventually mounting to a fever pitch. The pulsating rhythm seemed to tug at the masked participants, drawing them into the middle of the clearing where they began dancing emphatically, attempting to match the intensity of the musical blitz. They jerked their bodies, throwing themselves about wildly as if they were in a state of trance, yet their movements were synchronized perfectly. The dancers encircled Dumisai while moving their bodies excitedly to the syncopated beat of the drummers. The session continued at an exhausting pace for several minutes until finally the circle opened, allowing another dancer to enter their space. Dumisai watched with keen interest as the newest dancer faced him in the circle. Unlike the others, the newest dancer was wearing the *Pwevo* mask. Dumisai wondered about the significance of the dancer confronting him. He knew the *Pwevo* was intended to portray the beauty, grace and wisdom of the sacred woman. The mask was very stylized, displaying narrow slits for eyes which were set in large sockets and enhancing the soft contour of its facial features. Though it was customary for men to perform the ritual dance of the *Pwevo*, the dancer's movements so expertly mimicked that of a woman skilled in the art of dance that Dumisai easily succumbed to the hypnotic spell cast by the combination of rhythmic percussion and artful moves. Her movements were nimble and free, yet gentle and controlled, complementing the moves of the other *Makishi* dancers with grace and elegance. As she came closer to Dumisai, the music from the drums began to fade into a soft background ambiance.

The other dancers continued their synchronized movement which had slowed considerably so as not to distract from the focus of the ritual. Dumisai was oblivious to all save the *Pwevo* who had so masterfully captured his attention. Suddenly, the drumming resumed at full force. The loud and frenetic pulse of the rhythm seemed to take control of Dumisai's body, spinning him around and causing his outstretched arms to flail freely in the air. As the pace of the drumming increased, so did the speed of his turns. The music became a blur as he spun around deliriously in a single spot. Then the music suddenly stopped. Dumisai ceased spinning immediately in his tracks, as though his actions were being completely controlled by the drumming. He remained perfectly still, staring aimlessly into space as if he had temporarily lost touch with reality. The glaze over his eyes eventually faded as his vision began to slowly come back into focus, revealing many unfamiliar faces all around him. In his partial stupor, he thought he recognized Niangi's wife among the faces in the crowd. Before he could confirm whether or not it was the same woman, he felt his body beginning to get heavy. Immediately, he started to shake as his eyelids fluttered uncontrollably. He could feel his body becoming limp as his knees began to buckle and then finally, he collapsed.

Dumisai was unable to move as he lay stiff on the ground, unsure how long he had been lying there. Eventually, he attempted to slowly open his eyes but could not tolerate the blinding white light that permeated his surroundings. He was forced to squeeze his eyelids shut just to keep the blinding brightness at bay. Again, he tried peeking through his eyelids, this time using his hands to help shield his eyes from the light. The brightness had faded just enough, allowing Dumisai to finally tolerate the brilliant radiance of the light that had totally engulfed him. He sat up, still squinting as he looked around attentively, attempting to make sense of the pristine view that surrounded him. There was nothing but white light as far as he could see. With nowhere to go, Dumisai picked himself up off the ground and began walking. He wandered aimlessly at first, searching the distance for the horizon or any sign of life that might possibly exist. Finally, a break in the light appeared. It seemed to be fraying at the ends, becoming white streaks which trailed off into darkness. Before he could determine what was happening, most of the white light suddenly vanished. It had been replaced by the soft, wispy streaks of a nebulous cloud-like substance that was far away but still clearly visible. The cloud formation was shaped like a circular disc which brought to mind some cosmic whirlpool whose movement had somehow become suspended against the black backdrop of space. Sprinkled throughout the spiraling nebula were star clusters alternating between streaks of winding dust lanes. At its center was a bright yellow nucleus radiating light outward into the surrounding abyss. Except for the spiral formation, Dumisai was suddenly and completely abandoned to the desolate void of space where his body was left to float aimlessly through the unbounded expanse as if some mysterious power was in charge of directing his odyssey. He drifted away from the disc-shaped billow until he eventually noticed several more spiral formations scattered throughout the vast black chasm surrounding him. He was stunned by the sheer beauty of the heavenly formations. The magnificent cosmic designs were decorated with tiny spheres of bright light. Each one a unique example of spectacular artistry as if it had been purposely placed there on display by a master artisan showcasing his craft. Dumisai marveled at the sight which had captivated his attention with its breathtaking beauty. After several moments of being suspended in wonder, a slight force began to tug gently at his body as though it was beckoning for him to return. Even though he did not want to leave, he didn't offer any resistance. He allowed the gentle force to guide his movement on to some unknown destination. He could feel his body being drawn closer to one of the spiraling nebulae. Many of the tiny spheres of light sprinkled throughout the formation were quickly becoming large objects that were composed of spectacular colors. Before Dumisai could determine exactly what was happening, he noticed several wispy tufts of white clouds darting quickly past his sight. One of the globular objects had suddenly become massive. He braced for impact as he realized how quickly it was approaching from beneath. Several long moments passed before he touched down, gently coming to rest upon the terrain. Dumisai could finally feel the firm support of the ground beneath his feet again.

Immediately, the white light returned with a blinding flash, completely blotting out his vision. Surprisingly, his eyes seemed to adjust to the light quickly this time, allowing him to see sooner than he expected. The light began to change, becoming a bright mixture of yellow and orange that swirled in an obscure fog, inhibiting Dumisai's ability to see. In an effort to make it out of the fog-like cloud, he attempted to feel his way through the brume but his body did not respond. His inability to command his body to act surprised him. He re-checked his control over his limbs by attempting to raise his hands but noticed that they were not there. Dumisai looked around anxiously, searching for any part of his body. It was completely gone. The revelation came as a shock, almost causing him to panic. He stopped for a moment, attempting to collect his wits as he assessed what had happened. Perhaps he had become invisible. It was the only possible explanation, irrespective of logic. The sensations he experienced in the place of his missing extremities convinced him that he must still have a body even if it could not be seen. It was as though an illusory phantom of residual energy had been left in the wake of his body's disappearance. He could not see or touch it, yet it seemed real in every other way. He tried making the energy respond to his command but was unsuccessful. The setback was unnerving. The thought of not having a body prompted him to momentarily question his sanity even as something within his being urged him to let go of the emotional attachment that he had to the physical form. Dumisai briefly contemplated the thought which had managed to creep into his consciousness. The idea was intriguing. It had come as if a silent suggestion had been secretly whispered into his mind, informing him of an alternate reality that existed within a realm of untapped potential. As Dumisai mulled over the idea, he could not deny the truth of what had been suggested. Finally, he relented, embracing the idea and discarding the uncertainty that had kept him attached to his physical senses. The act was liberating, freeing him from the thoughts and sensations which had kept him tied to the phantom resonance. The mental impressions which had once filled his mind quickly dissolved into an airy flux of ethers. The whole process awakened something slumbering deep within his spirit, gently arousing some secret dormant forces that he was unaware even existed.

He could feel their power beginning to surge within as though a million tiny pin pricks were urgently disturbing the quiet of his existence. His consciousness was flooded with a sea of astral energies. He bathed in the ethereal brume, allowing it to completely overwhelm his senses. The sensation threw him into a state of ecstatic trance, rendering him incapable of differentiating his own thoughts from the stream of ideation that is cosmic consciousness. His mind seemed to be expanding, merging with the collective consciousness of the universe itself. The connection was intoxicating, propelling him to a state of euphoric bliss. For a brief moment he was one with all, displaced in the tempestuous swirl of energy that was taking him to the brink of delirium.

Dumisai had lost all sense of time when the tumult finally subsided. The flux had transformed into a state of peaceful tranquility. He retreated into the void of beatific peace while simply observing the cosmic dance unfolding in the heavens all around him. He had become aware of all activity occurring within the continuum of energy that permeated the cosmos. Eventually, he detected a fervent stirring within the energy field again. He could feel the movement amongst the scattered celestial forces as they started to swirl, building to a state of agitated restlessness that continued for several minutes before finally coalescing into a giant ball. It was as though the entire process was being guided by some invisible intelligence that was responsible for marshalling it into an ever-expanding mass. The cosmic confection assimilated everything in its path, causing the concentrated forces to reach critical-mass before finally exploding into a dazzling display of light and colors. The explosion lit up the whole of space in a blinding flash that stretched as far as the eye could see. After several seconds of illuminated silence, the brilliance began to fade, revealing an earth-like terrain covered with lush, green vegetation. It was a scene of incredible beauty which continued for miles. The landscape was picturesque and filled with various species of animals roaming freely across the countryside. A group of birds frolicked carelessly in the gentle respite of morning air. Several fish took turns dancing across the top of a mountain stream before disappearing again beneath the water's surface. Dumisai looked out on the panoramic vista consisting of snow-capped mountain ranges, waterfalls and green meadows. The unspoiled landscape was exactly as he had imagined life on earth would look if everything was in perfect harmony. He was sure that he had found paradise. The sight left him in awe as he took in the incomparable beauty of creation. The urge to experience the idyllic beauty of the entire world was impossible to resist.

The scenery had captured Dumisai's attention like some entranced spectator. He was so enthralled that he almost did not notice the body of a dead animal which was lying in plain sight on the ground. The aberration came as a complete shock, forcing him to withdraw his senses back into the physical plane of existence. He zoomed in, focusing on the animal whose carcass was still surrounded by an striking display of exceptional beauty. It appeared to be the remains of a buffalo decomposing in the heat of the sun. Several vultures appeared out of nowhere and circled overhead. Dumisai was dismayed by the sight but attempted to remain optimistic, telling himself that the death was only part of the natural cycle of life. Still, something about what he had seen did not sit right. He ignored the negative thought that came to his mind, choosing instead to focus on the surrounding beauty.

Immediately, he noticed another fallen buffalo. The vultures had not even discovered the remains of this most recent death. This second sighting unnerved Dumisai. It was confirmation of his suspicion that something was not quite right. He was unsure of what to expect next as dark clouds began forming in the distance. The sky had become a hazy and dismal shade of gray. All around, the bodies of more dead animals became visible and were scattered across the plains. The number of dead animals dotting the landscape seemed to outnumber those that were alive. The sky was becoming increasingly dark, aided by billowing plumes of black smoke rising above the adjacent forest. It was evident that fire had transformed the once flourishing vegetation into a scorched field of burnt charcoal. He could see that animals were attempting to flee the area in a panic-stricken terror. Others struggled to escape the destruction but were unable to do so because of an oily, black muck which covered their bodies. On the horizon, the outline of several buildings jutting into the sky was barely visible. Dumisai was hesitant, afraid of what new discovery awaited him there, yet his curiosity would not allow him to turn away without investigating. The moment he arrived, he spotted the lifeless body of an adolescent youth lying face down and riddled with bullets. It was an eerie scene, yet the sight of a dead body lying in the middle of the rain-soaked warehouse parking lot seemed almost predictable given the circumstance of the surroundings. The scene removed any remaining doubts that something had gone terribly wrong. It was as if a view into a dark reality had been opened up, revealing a world that had been cast into a cycle of chaos and despair.

The harsh reality bombarded Dumisai, projecting an endless stream of violence and murder for him to witness firsthand. It had become obvious that all of the death and suffering was leading to something catastrophic. Dumisai could barely stand to watch what was happening anymore. He longed for the return of the blissful feeling that he had previously experienced, but there was no escaping the unrelenting view into the misery of the world. Then, in an instant, all daylight vanished. The light was replaced by a complete and all-encompassing darkness that appeared as an endless expanse of thick, black fog. A tiny, lone star flickering brightly in the distance of the night sky was all that could be seen. The object quivered in defiance of the desolate darkness, as if trying to entice someone's attention to it. Dumisai was drawn to it, mesmerized by the luminosity of its unrelenting brilliance. At first it appeared to be coming closer until he saw that it was actually slowly increasing in size. As the object continued to grow, he realized that it was not a star, but rather a glowing, white orb whose pulsations managed to consistently illuminate a small portion of the surrounding darkness. Dumisai looked closely as the orb began to take shape. It quickly changed from a mass of shapeless light into a human form. He immediately recognized the form as the body of a young boy who could have been his identical twin. The vaguely familiar scene was sufficient to shock his memory, reminding him of the body that he no longer possessed but needed in order to maneuver in the physical realm. He noticed that the child was sitting peacefully in a meditative pose as seed-like particles of light began to radiate outward from its body. The light shined with supernatural brilliance until it had completely dispersed the entire expanse of darkness that had engulfed the miserable world. As the radiance removed the remaining remnants of the ruined earth by replacing the dead with new life forms, the fallen animals began to rise suddenly, embracing their opportunity for another chance to live. Dumisai suddenly realized the meaning of it all. The answer had come to him swiftly after witnessing the terrible fate that was waiting to befall the world. He now knew that he would have to return in order to help rescue the world from its ill-fated future. Though he did not want to return to a place of suffering, he knew that he must. Immediately, he could feel his own consciousness begin to withdraw from the field of primordial energy. He felt a tingling sensation returning to the location where his extremities were supposed to be. Without hesitation, he approached the meditating body and intentionally passed his consciousness into the physical form. The shock of acquiring a new body suddenly jolted him out of his trance. He emerged from the muse just as a dash of water splashed across his face.

Dumisai sat up abruptly, instinctively recoiling from the wet contact of the pungent smelling liquid which was now dripping from his brow. He looked around, still dazed and his arms slightly sore from flailing against the ground as he attempted to figure out what had happened to him. Immediately, he raised his hands in front of his face to examine and make sure that he was whole. Just beyond his reach, a man was standing directly in front of him holding an empty gourd. Dumisai recognized him as one of the drummers. As he slowly stood from his seated position on the ground, he noticed that the large gathering of people was still present. It was a mass of humanity that completely surrounded Dumisai. He wondered why he had become the center of so much attention, as if they were waiting to see what he would do next. He scanned the faces of as many people as he could quickly, hoping to identify someone that he might recognize. Finally, he spotted Ol' Manzalele among the many faces in the crowd. He remembered that she had been responsible for leading him there and maneuvered to get close enough to speak to her. He had only taken a couple steps before his path was suddenly blocked. Looking up, he saw the face of the masked *Pwevo* staring directly into his own. He waited, unsure what to do next. The masked dancer continued its piercing stare before finally deciding to slowly remove the ritual mask. Dumisai felt the beat of his heart quicken as he eagerly waited for the dancer to reveal its identity. After a seemingly endless moment, the mask was finally lowered, revealing the face of the person. Dumisai gasped a speechless breath before managing to regain his composure.

"Gr–Grandma…? Grandma Lueji??" Dumisai stuttered. "Grandmother, is it really you?"

"IT IS I, DUMISAI. IT IS SO GOOD TO BE HERE AND TALK TO YOU AGAIN."

"Grandmother, how is it possible? You… Ol' Manzalele… how are you able…?"

"THROUGH OUR RITUALS AND TRADITIONS, SON. HAVEN'T I ALWAYS TOLD YOU THAT THESE THINGS ARE POSSIBLE?"

"Yes, Grandmother, I did believe you, but…"

"I KNOW YOU DID, SON. YOU HAVE LEARNED WELL."

"Grandmother, I missed you … can you stay? Please don't leave again. I want you to stay with me."

"I AM ALWAYS WITH YOU, DUMISAI. HAVEN'T I TOLD YOU THAT?"

"Yes… ma'am," Dumisai agreed reluctantly, realizing the obvious implication of his grandmother's answer.

She paused as she looked out on the gathering of people. **"Dumisai, take a good look around you. What do you see?"**

"These people, Grandmother—who are they?"

"These are your ancestors, Dumisai."

"Yes, I remember now," he replied after recalling his journey to the bottom of the river. "I've been here before, then."

"Yes, Dumisai, you have been here before, but this time you have come with a different purpose."

"What do you mean, Grandmother?"

"Dumisai, what you see assembled before you are the ancestors whom you shall carry with you from this day forward."

"I do not understand."

"I know, son. That is why we brought you here—to help you understand. We have been telling you all along that we are with you, ready to provide guidance from the inner planes, yet you still doubt. Dumisai, you cannot allow doubt to undermine the power that has been entrusted to you. You have to know that you are dealing in truth!"

"Grandmother, I do believe it. I have always believed what you've told me."

"Dumisai, can't you see that that is the problem? Belief is no good! You are still relying on belief when you should be knowing! Son, it is important that you understand what is at stake—you are about to undertake a task that will mark your entry into a spiritual war which is being fought for the very soul of this world. The hopes and aspirations of millions of people depend on you. Do you understand that?"

"Yes, I understand, but it just seems like so much."

"SON, I KNOW IT IS A LOT TO ASK, BUT YOU DO NOT HAVE TO BEAR THIS BURDEN ALONE. THAT'S WHY WE ARE HERE—SO THAT YOU WILL KNOW THAT WE ARE READY TO ASSIST WHEN YOU NEED US."

"Grandmother, what if I fail?"

"DUMISAI, THERE IS NO FAILURE AS LONG AS YOU STRIVE TO DO WHAT IS RIGHT AND LIVE TRUTH. NOW THAT YOU HAVE SEEN THE FACE OF GOD, YOU KNOW WHAT IS REQUIRED. YOUR TRAINING HAS PREPARED YOU, NOW YOU HAVE TO TAKE ALL THAT YOU HAVE LEARNED INTO THE WORLD."

"Yes ma'am," he said as he wondered what she had in store for him.

"DUMISAI, COME CLOSER, SON."

As Dumisai stepped forward, he noticed that the ancestors had gathered close around him. He could see a white light beginning to radiate from the surrounding circle of deceased beings. It was as though a field of electrical current had charged the atmosphere, saturating the night air with potent energy. Suddenly, the entire gathering of ancestors began to transform, becoming an ethereal mist of ghostly apparitions. The spirit-beings swirled benevolently through the clearing before finally streaming into the scar tissue of the X-shaped laceration that had been carved above Dumisai's heart. As the center of his chest began to glow with incandescent light, the area surrounding the scar began to burn the outline of a strange design into his skin. Within moments, the light faded, leaving the diamond-shaped *Chin-gel-yen-gel-ye* symbol etched onto the center of his chest. Dumisai could still feel the power which was surging through his body, illuminating the *Chin-gel-yen-gel-ye* mark and causing it to radiate a soft glow that could be seen through the cloth of his shirt. As the final streams of ancestral rays finished assimilating into his body, only Lueji was left standing before him. Dumisai was awash in energy as he reveled in the experience. He felt wiser now. It was as though he was suddenly able to see through the eyes of several generations of ancestors that had come before him and draw upon their personal experiences as if they were his own.

"Grandmother, I understand now," he said as if a profound insight had been suddenly revealed to him.

"GOOD, DUMISAI, YOU NOW CARRY THE LIGHT OF WISDOM THAT COMES FROM YOUR ANCESTORS. WE HAVE BECOME YOU, AND YOU, US! THE TIME HAS FINALLY COME, MY SON. ARE YOU READY TO MEET YOUR DESTINY?"

"Yes, Grandmother, I am ready."

"GOOD—THEN IT IS TIME FOR YOU TO LEAVE THIS WORLD OF SPIRIT AND RETURN TO YOUR OWN, FOR THERE IS MUCH WORK TO DO."

"Grandmother, do you have to leave?"

"YES, SON," she comforted while giving him a final hug, **"BUT I AM ALWAYS WITH YOU."** Dumisai watched as Lueji stepped back and then transformed her spirit-body into a ghost-like mist. As she entered the talisman adorning his neck, it glowed softly, emitting a bluish hue as the energy poured into it. Dumisai could feel the energy emanating from the black onyx stone and pulsing briefly against his body before finally passing into the *Chin-gel-yen-gel-ye* mark under his shirt. After Lueji was gone, Dumisai felt a strange sensation wash over him before suddenly realizing that he was surrounded by pitch blackness. It had only been a momentary lapse in awareness before he recognized the cascading moonlight and the soft rhythm of the drumbeat slowly creeping back into his consciousness. The pace of the drumming seemed subdued now. It was only ambient noise to Dumisai, who was still basking in the afterglow of his encounter with the ancestors. Except for the drummers, the entire area was completely vacant. He still wished that he had had more time to spend with his grandmother, but he could at least take comfort in knowing that she would always be nearby. As he stood in the middle of the clearing, the light from the moon cast a large shadow off of his body. On the periphery of his vision he noticed the *Pwevo* mask still lying on the ground next to his shadow. Satisfied that he had not imagined the evening's events, Dumisai retrieved the mask to place on his father's shrine and then returned to his parent's hut where he settled in for the remainder of the night.

EPILOGUE

An inconspicuous energy stirred recklessly in the dimly lit corridor. Its subtle movement would have been completely undetectable had it not been for the flickering particles of dust floating aimlessly in a trickle of light filtering through a dirty window. The glimmer of light seemed to retreat from the dark recesses of the long, winding corridor, either unable or unwilling to penetrate the thickness of the dark and musty air that surrounded it. The energy stirred slowly at first, apparently waiting for an opportune time to mobilize into a sustainable force. Several seemingly incessant flashes of lightning illuminated the drizzling rainfall on the doleful night, followed by the rumblings of thunder which reverberated loudly through the midnight air. The electrical discharges seemed to stop only long enough for the cycle to repeat itself. Even the vivid flashes of light could not stave off the persistent darkness still stalking the corridor. The discharges of electricity in the atmosphere appeared to be feeding the stirring energy, aiding and abetting the nurturing of its strength. Finally, it was strong enough to deliberately propel itself down the hallway, gathering speed as it moved, sweeping around each of the corners of the adjoining rooms. The growing force was able to maneuver with intention as it swept down the long corridor leading into the basement of the adjoining building and brushing past a young man standing just inside the doorway.

JoJo looked around nervously, attempting to identify the source of the strange sensation that swept over him. He wasn't able to put his finger on it, but he knew something had changed. Being in the room just didn't feel right. Every instinctive impulse within his being screamed for him to get out of there, but he knew that was not an option. He may as well have signed his own death certificate if he'd let on that he didn't want to be down with the Clique anymore. Even before experiencing the strange feeling, the idea of meeting in the old abandoned warehouse at midnight had made him uneasy. He had argued that they should ambush the 8Treys out in the open, but Big Mike wouldn't go for it. Big Mike had something to prove. He wanted to teach the 8Trey Gangstas a lesson by luring them out to the building and then making an example out of them. JoJo felt trapped. He knew someone was bound to die tonight but it was too late to worry about that now. He was in too deep. He was representing the 40Deuce Clique, and once in the Clique, always in the Clique. It didn't matter that he had only recently just turned thirteen. Now it was time for him to put in some work and show his homeboys that he was ready to die if necessary. They had a lookout posted across the street in another building communicating updates by walkie-talkie. A warning from the lookout that the 8Treys were starting to pull up in force helped JoJo refocus his attention. He made his way to the window anxiously to try to get a glimpse of how many had come. A burst of lightning briefly lit up the night sky. JoJo almost jumped when a frantic yell suddenly came over the walkie-talkie. He tried to quickly regroup without revealing that he had been startled by the lookout yelling into the walkie-talkie.

"Hey... slow down, man... we can't understand nothin' you saying!" JoJo called back while stepping back from the window for safety.

"WHAT WAS THAT!?!" the lookout yelled into the walkie-talkie, the volume of his voice distorting the sound.

"What?" JoJo inquired, looking around anxiously. "What do you see? Is it da 8Treys? Where they at??!"

"Naw, this won't no 8Treys. This won't even no person. This was something else!"

"Look bruh," Big Mike warned, speaking into the walkie-talkie, "we got business to handle. Now ain't the time to be playing. You understand me?!? You better jus keep an eye on them 8Treys and let us know what they do'in!"

"Big Mike, I swear, man, I know I saw something. It's in there wit y'all!" the lookout reiterated.

Everyone began checking around nervously, looking at each other and searching for anything that seemed out of place. Big Mike could sense that the situation was starting to get out of hand.

"Look, ain't nothing in here," he declared, brandishing his gun to reassert his control. A quick succession of gunfire mingled with a dreadful moan suddenly came over the walkie-talkie. Immediately, the sound of a crashing noise followed, and then the walkie-talkie went silent.

"Lil' Mo...? LIL' MO!!!?" Big Mike yelled, hoping for an answer that, deep down, he already knew wasn't coming.

Everyone from the 40Deuce Clique was starting to become frantic. Things were not going according to plan.

Glancing out the window, they could see several 8Trey Gangstas starting to pour into the building. Big Mike knew that they had to get out of the basement before it became their deathtrap. He signaled for everyone to scatter as they scrambled down the corridor. If they could reach the open floor of the warehouse, they would be able spread out and find some cover. JoJo could hear the 8Treys coming in their direction. He tried not to listen to their gunfire as he ran frantically for cover. He knew that they were trying to create a sense of panic among him and his homeboys, but it was impossible for him to contain his fear.

The gun battle that ensued raged intensely, causing the energy to pulse even more violently as it fed off of the heightened emotions of the combatants. Finally, the energy was strong enough to morph from a fluid, shapeless mass into something with a definite form. Big Mike was a born leader. He calmly directed the 40Deuce Clique as they managed to push the 8Treys back toward the building's entrance. The sound of blazing guns continued with only the flash from their muzzles providing any visible target to aim the return fire. The rain was pouring down now more forcefully than ever, while the thunder and lightning boomed violently overhead. JoJo was trying to maintain his composure but his adrenaline was pumping nearly out of control. He wasn't ready to die yet, especially not for some gang or a meaningless reputation. He wasn't sure what he was doing there anyway. He desperately wished that he could go back in time and change his decision that had led to him joining the Clique. He knew that was only wishful thinking, but contemplated the possibility that his past bad choices did not have to dictate his future. He managed to find a large barrel to hide safely behind and waited for an opportunity to make his escape.

As he exhaled a momentary sigh of relief, the gunplay became a blur while thoughts of his early childhood transported him to a more sane time in his life. The memories of his early childhood brought a smile to his lips. He remembered sitting outside, enjoying a summer's visit down south and attempting to count the endless number of stars on a country night while passing the time with his mother's family. Unfortunately, his daydream did not last. The sound of a bullet glancing off of the barrel that he was hiding behind coincided with a brilliant flash of lightning, awaking him from the temporary escape of his daydream. As the dazzle from the lightning faded, he thought he noticed a stealthy silhouette hovering over the room like a deadly predator. Another bullet whizzed by his head, forcing him to refocus his attention on the deadly battle at hand. With the knowledge of what he thought he had seen temporarily dominating his awareness, he struggled to keep his attention on his enemies who were shooting at him. Another burst of lightning illuminated the room long enough for him to get a good view of the silhouetted form. It was like nothing he had seen before. It was larger than life with its long anteater shaped head and big, donkey-like ears. JoJo was frozen stiff with fear. He was oblivious to everything else happening around him. He could see the creature's blazing-red eyes staring down directly at him. JoJo panicked, dropping his gun and attempted to run from the building.

"JoJo, where you going?!?" one of his homeboys called out, unsure why his friend was deserting them.

JoJo didn't stop. In the confusion, he was able to somehow make it out the door into the parking lot. A series of non-stop, rapid-fire shots rang out from the inside of a vehicle waiting across the lot. JoJo made it only halfway across before the bullets cut him down. The creature shrieked in satisfaction. It's eerie shrill was immediately followed by a loud clap of thunder. Oblivious to the fate of their dead homey, the 40Deuce Clique continued their personal war with the 8Trey Gangstas. The creature relished in the maelstrom of violence that washed over the neglected area of the city, growing stronger while feeding off the conflict and destruction that raged in the area. Hundreds of miles away, Dumisai slept peacefully. A distinct, maddening shriek awakened him suddenly, causing him to sit up abruptly from his restful sleep. A rush of images flooded his mind's eye, allowing him to briefly witness the onslaught of evil in the world. The vision of an avenging red dragon emitting a bright, purplish hue pushed back the darkness attempting to engulf the world, finally forcing it into a black hole. Dumisai looked around briefly before getting up to check outside his window. The promise of a new day beckoned on the horizon.

FIN

Glossary of Terms

Áfu – Spirit of a deceased ancestor who returns to the world to guide, assist, protect and educate members of the community on important occasions.

Akishi – Masked character representing the spirit of a deceased ancestor who has returned to the world of the living to guide, assist and protect the village during times of importance. Pronounced "a-KEY-shee". *(Plural: Makishi)*.

Albino – A person born with deficient pigmentation (color) in their skin, hair and eyes. Often the skin is of a milky hue and the eyes are pink.

Angola – A country in Southwest Africa bordered by the Atlantic Ocean, Zambia, Namibia and the Democratic Republic of Congo (formerly Zaire). Angola gained independence from Portugal colonization in 1975but fought a brutal civil war between 1975 and 2002.

Astral Body – A type of spirit form believed to coexist with the human physical body.

Chingelyengelye – A diamond-shaped geometric pattern used among the Chokwe and related people. The pattern has a triangle on each corner and symbolizes a sacred connection to the divine principle. Some historians claim that the symbol came into use based upon contact with the Portuguese, however, there is no evidence to substantiate that claim. Pronounced "chen-gel-yen-GEL-yeh".

Chikunza – A sacred mask used by the Chokwe to symbolize power and authority. Pronounced "chee-KHUN-zah".

Chokwe – A prominent tribe and ethnic group in Angola. Members also reside in the bordering countries of Zambia and the Democratic Republic of Congo.

Civil War – A war that is fought between different factions within the same country.

Colonization – The process by which one country controls the land and resources of another country.

Congo *(Democratic Republic of Congo)* – A country in Central Africa which gained its independence from Belgium colonization in 1960. Formerly Congo Free State, Belgian Congo, and Zaire.

Cowrie Shells – A white or brightly marked shell used for divination or currency in parts of Africa.

Diviner – One who has the ability to foretell future events by supernatural means.

Divination – The art of foretelling future events or revealing occult knowledge by a supernatural agency such as an oracle.

Emaciated – Extremely thin, especially as a result of malnutrition or starvation.

Immigrant – A person entering a country for the purpose of permanent residence.

Egypt – A country in northeast Africa famous for its ancient monuments and historic civilization.

Emigrant – A person who leaves a country or region to relocate in another.

Enigma – Something that cannot be satisfactorily explained.

Expatriate – A person who voluntarily leaves or is forcefully removed from their native country to become a citizen of another.

FNLA – *(National Front for the Liberation of Angola)* Revolutionary political party that fought to liberate Angola from the colonial rule of Portugal.

Initiation – A ceremony, ritual, test, or period of instruction with which a new member is admitted to an organization or body of knowledge.

Katanga *(Shaba)* – A province of present day Democratic Republic of Congo which borders Angola and Zambia. The area attempted to break away from the country (Zaire) immediately after its independence from Belgium. Today, the province is known as Shaba.

Leopold – A King of Belgium who is credited with colonizing and establishing the *Congo Free State* in 1885 but which is known today as the *Democratic Republic of Congo*. King Leopold is known for the brutality with which he ruled the Congo, amassing millions of dollars in personal fortune at the expense of millions of lives of the Congolese people.

MPLA – *(Popular Movement for the Liberation of Angola)* Revolutionary political party that fought to liberate Angola from the colonial rule of Portugal.

Mukanda – A manhood initiation ritual among the Chokwe and related ethnic groups of Angola, Zambia, and Congo for boys that have come of age. The process usually took place during the dry season and lasted for several months. Pronounced "mu-KHAN-dah".

Ndebele *(Matabele)* –An ethnic group of modern day Zimbabwe. The group split from the Zulus of South Africa in the 1820's and re-settled in modern day Zimbabwe. Pronounced "n-deh-BEH-le".

N'ganga – A traditional healer or Diviner among the Chokwe and related ethnic groups. Sometimes consulted to counteract evil spirits or illnesses.

Ngoma – A goatskin-covered drum used in celebrations and for communication purposes.

Oklahoma – One of the 50 states that make up the United States of America. Located in the south central region of the USA and is bordered primarily by Texas, Kansas and Arkansas.

Occult – Relating to supernatural influences and phenomena.

Oracle – A person or medium through which one can talk to God to receive a divine communication or revelation.

Portugal – A country located in southwest Europe which colonized Angola and Brazil.

Portuguese – Primary language spoken by the people of Portugal, Angola and Brazil.

Pwevo *(Pwo)* – An ancestral reference representative of the archetypical woman among the Chokwe people, often represented by a mask. Pronounced "PWEH-vo".

Reservation – A parcel of land that was reserved for the Native American Indian tribes after being forced to move from their ancestral land by the U.S. Government.

Ritual – A detailed method of procedure for performing a religious ceremony.

Rites of Passage – A ritual or ceremony signifying an event in a person's life indicating a transition from one stage to another such as from adolescence to manhood.

Sorcerer – A person who seeks to control and use the forces of nature or magic powers.

Subconscious – The part of the mind below the level of conscious perception.

Tundanji – The title given to Mukanda initiates while they are away at the initiation camp. Pronounced "toon-DHAN-jee".

UNITA – *(National Union for the Total Independence of Angola)* Political organization and revolutionary movement in Angola which initially began fighting to overthrow Portuguese colonial rule, then later fought the Angolan government led by the MPLA.

Wanga – Evil spirits or supernatural elements among the Chokwe and related ethnic groups that may be called upon by sorcerers for specific purposes.

Zambia – A country in Southern Africa which gained its independence from colonization by England in 1964. Formerly Northern Rhodesia.

Zimbabwe – A country in Southern Africa which gained its independence from colonization by England in 1985. Formerly Rhodesia.

ABOUT THE AUTHOR

Christopher R. Obie was born and raised on a farm in North Carolina where he gained a tremendous respect and appreciation for all of nature. In addition to working in the Computer Science field, Christopher loves reading, writing, drawing and raising his four kids.

www.ingramcontent.com/pod-product-compliance
Lightning Source LLC
Chambersburg PA
CBHW021242260626
47155CB00004BA/1265